W9-AVY-041

"What *happened* in here?"

Marc gazed around the kitchen in obvious horror. There was chocolate on every single surface.

"We were making cookies. I, uh, was just going to clean up." As Leah grabbed a dishcloth and began to wipe the counter, a stray slip of paper fell to the floor. She unfolded it and read the three awkwardly printed words.

"LEAH LOVE MARC"

Marc reached over and plucked the note from her fingers before she had a chance to crumple it. Arching an eyebrow, he muttered, "Would you like to explain this? Or does the message speak for itself?"

Leah felt like crawling under a cupboard. "I was teaching Ariana some new words," she replied tersely. "I—I guess she was practicing them."

"What other words did you teach her?"

"None. Just those. Not . . . not in that order, though!"

Judy Kaye, a voracious reader throughout her childhood, still likes to "get lost in a good story, a well-planned fantasy"—but these days, that usually means she's writing it herself. She's a much-published author of romances, mysteries and young-adult fiction. *Ariana's Magic* is her second Harlequin Romance novel. Judy lives in North Dakota with her husband (her "real-life hero"), two daughters and one cat (who sleeps on her desk while she types).

Books by Judy Kaye

HARLEQUIN ROMANCE
3021—LETTERS OF LOVE

Don't miss any of our special offers. Write to us at the following address for information on our newest releases.

Harlequin Reader Service
P.O. Box 1397, Buffalo, NY 14240
Canadian address: P.O. Box 603,
Fort Erie, Ont. L2A 5X3

ARIANA'S MAGIC
Judy Kaye

Harlequin Books

TORONTO • NEW YORK • LONDON
AMSTERDAM • PARIS • SYDNEY • HAMBURG
STOCKHOLM • ATHENS • TOKYO • MILAN

ISBN 0-373-03182-3

Harlequin Romance first edition March 1992

ARIANA'S MAGIC

Copyright © 1992 by Judy Baer.
All rights reserved. Except for use in any review, the reproduction or utilization
of this work in whole or in part in any form by any electronic, mechanical or
other means, now known or hereafter invented, including xerography,
photocopying and recording, or in any information storage or retrieval system,
is forbidden without the permission of the publisher, Harlequin Enterprises
Limited, 225 Duncan Mill Road, Don Mills, Ontario, Canada M3B 3K9.

All the characters in this book have no existence outside the imagination of
the author and have no relation whatsoever to anyone bearing the same name
or names. They are not even distantly inspired by any individual known or
unknown to the author, and all incidents are pure invention.

® are Trademarks registered in the United States Patent and Trademark Office
and in other countries.

Printed in U.S.A.

CHAPTER ONE

Adams, Forester and Grant, Attorneys-at-Law.

Leah Brock's stomach engaged in a series of flip-flops and her palms grew sticky as she read the names backward through the office door's frosted glass.

Suddenly the door at the far side of the room swung open, revealing an imposing man, well over six feet tall, broad-shouldered and elegant in a finely tailored navy suit with a scarlet tie. His dark eyes scanned the room and settled impersonally on Leah. "Ms. Brock? Will you come in?" He closed the office doors behind them and turned to study her. Mesmerized, Leah stared back.

"I'm Marc Adams." As his large warm hand engulfed her dainty one, Leah felt her fingertips sizzling as though she'd brushed them, wet, over a hot griddle.

His hair was black, relieved only by the barest hint of brown. A single unruly lock fell over his forehead and grazed one arched eyebrow. His skin was bronzed, his features even, his expression intense.

"So you're the nanny the agency recommends I hire." His inflection implied that he'd made the mistake of buying horseflesh sight unseen.

"I hope I'm acceptable," she replied dryly.

He placed his hands on the arms of his chair and sank into it with a world-weary sigh. "You're a lovely woman, Ms. Brock. I'm sure you'd be very acceptable under most circumstances. Unfortunately you appear to be rather…young for my purposes.'' His gaze was clinical as he folded his arms across his chest. ''Tell me about yourself. Convince me that it's in my best interest to employ you.''

''I'm a college graduate. Summa cum laude. I have a master's degree in special education and I minored in business management. I love children and I'm very good with them.'' Leah lowered her jade-flecked eyes and absently tucked her hair behind her ear. Then she plunged into the explanation that might end the job agreement on the spot. ''I want to open my own nanny placement agency here in Washington—a specialized service for families with handicapped children. I'm looking for a temporary position in order to gain firsthand experience.''

''Very admirable, Ms. Brock, but what good will that do me?'' Adams's eyebrow disappeared beneath that dark, wayward lock. ''You're not looking for a permanent position. Eventually I'll have to hire another nanny. Don't you think that would be disruptive for your charge?''

Her charge. Ariana Adams. The agency had given Leah few details about the girl other than her age and the fact that her family was highly exacting when it came to her care.

''I realize that, but I wanted to be honest with you about my situation. It's important that I have experience as a nanny in order to run my own business with understanding and compassion.''

''What *do* you know about day-to-day living with the handicapped?''

A faint smile tugged at the corners of Leah's lips and a dimple flickered in one cheek. ''I come from a very close family. My nearest and dearest cousin is a Down Syndrome child. Mary stays with us every summer on our family farm in Wisconsin. She's the reason I want to start my own agency.''

Adams's expression softened. ''A Down Syndrome child?''

"Yes, and one of the most loving, beautiful people I know."

An indefinable emotion played across his features. Abruptly he leaned forward and closed the appointment book on his desk. "I think, Ms. Brock, that I'll give you an opportunity to prove yourself."

"Just like that?" Leah was astonished by the unexpected turnabout.

He pulled a slip of paper from the inside pocket of his suit coat. "Here are phone numbers and names with which you should acquaint yourself. Ariana's physician, Dr. Carmichael. Her dentist, nutritionist, seamstress and so on. Mrs. Bright, my housekeeper, has a copy. We can discuss her schedule when you arrive tomorrow. Routine is very important for Ariana—but I'm sure you understand that. Since the agency recommended you, I trust everything will be satisfactory." His appealing smile caught Leah off guard, unprepared for the antics of her thudding heart.

He produced a business card. "Here are my office phone numbers. The one on the back is my private line. If there's ever any problem with Ariana you are to call me immediately. *Immediately.* Do you understand?"

"Of course, but I do have some questions that need to be answered." She'd been trained to consider the big picture—overall progress—not to worry about details. Following schedules and adhering to rules were not her strong suits.

"Isn't tomorrow soon enough?" Marc Adams frowned impatiently.

"I, uh, sense that our methods of child care are quite different." Leah preferred a free-spirited approach to life, an attitude that stemmed from her rural family-oriented background. "I think we should discuss them now to avoid any misunderstanding. If you could let me know more about your daughter—"

His attractive lips pressed together in a tight line. "Ariana is my sister, not my daughter. She's seventeen. I'm divorced and have no children of my own. I assumed you'd been briefed." He visibly resigned himself to explaining. "Our parents died four years ago. A car-train crash in Scotland. It was their first vacation since Ariana's birth. The first and last."

His voice, which had been so impassive, filled with undeniable sadness. "Ariana was born when my mother was forty-four, seventeen years after me. I barely knew her when she was a young child because I was away at school. Now she's my responsibility. I returned home so Ariana's life wouldn't be disrupted any more than necessary." He sighed, his expression stoic. "Fortunately my mother was always very specific about what should and shouldn't be done for my sister's welfare. In that sense, she made it easy for me to enter the void and provide Ariana's care."

"I'm sorry about your parents," Leah said sincerely. "And I'm anxious to meet your sister."

A smile appeared, and Leah noticed the way his eyes crinkled, noticed the network of tiny lines that radiated from their corners. Marc Adams was a very attractive man.

"Ariana is a lovely girl, good-natured and charming. But as my law practice grows, I have less and less time to spend at home with her, and Mrs. Bright can only handle so much. You do have fine academic credentials," he said, looking dubiously at the file in front of him, "but do you feel you have enough experience to handle this?"

"Just because my cousin Mary isn't on my résumé doesn't mean I lack experience. In fact, I'd like to discuss some ideas I have for—"

"It'll have to be tomorrow. I've got a client arriving in ten minutes." His voice lowered in warning. "Ms. Brock, although you may have new concepts you'd like to implement, remember that Ariana is perfectly happy with her life as it is now." He shoved the folder to one side. "I'd like to be at the house when you arrive. Shall we say two-thirty?"

Leah knew she'd been dismissed. The ideas she had wanted to present would have to come later when the time was right. She bobbed her head in agreement and backed toward the door.

Outside she clasped her hands together with glee.

The job was hers! She'd taken one small step toward one very large dream.

COWARD. Leah stared at the brass knocker on the raised oak panel of Marc Adams's impressive front door. In fact, the whole house was impressive, even for this wealthy Bethesda neighborhood. It was a cockeyed notion to hire herself out as a nanny. Surely she could have opened a nanny placement agency without subjecting herself to this! Unsteadily she raised the knocker, then dropped it. She heard the thud reverberate through the interior of the house like a thundering cannon.

The sound had barely stopped when Marc appeared. He wore another suit of dark wool, a pristine white shirt and a deep red tie—a power suit. He hardly needed it. She suspected that Marc Adams would have been just as potent in rags. "There you are!" He gestured toward the Rolex on his wrist. "You're late."

Leah glanced at her own watch. Two thirty-one. One minute after the appointed time.

He guided her into a foyer, which was as large and imposing as Leah had imagined it would be. The floor tile was an opulent burgundy, with a peacock-feather motif in the center.

"May I take your coat?"

As her fingers worked the buttons, Leah took in the immaculate interior of the house. Every detail, every fabric, every texture bespoke wealth, yet there was an almost painful orderliness about the place.

A heavyset woman appeared in the doorway at the far end of the hall. Behind her, Leah could see a gleaming white kitchen. "Sorry, sir," the woman said. "I would have answered the door, but I was checking my cake."

"It's quite all right." He smiled, and the hint of a dimple slashed his cheek. "Mrs. Bright, this is Ms. Brock. Ariana's been waiting eagerly to meet her."

Leah refused to apologize for being tardy. If he'd looked out the window at twenty-five past the hour, he would have seen her on his steps trying to convince herself she wasn't nervous. Now she knew she'd had every right to be!

Leah relinquished her trench coat to Mrs. Bright, feeling vulnerable and silly in the dowdy gray uniform the agency had insisted she wear. She smoothed the front of her dress and glanced at her employer, who was looking at her with distaste. As their eyes met, a politely distant expression slid over his features. "I'd like to introduce you to Ariana, Ms. Brock. Please come into the living room."

Though it was mid-May, a fire burned in the fireplace. There were several vases of fresh flowers and a collection of exquisitely framed brass rubbings hung on one wall. Soft background music drifted from concealed speakers, but it was the tinkling of a piano that drew Leah's attention. A blond teenage girl sat at the baby grand in the far corner, her back toward the room, tapping out a tuneless melody.

"Ariana, there's someone here I'd like you to meet."

The girl turned abruptly and stared at them. Her face was round and full, her straight hair the color of pale sunlight and her intense blue eyes a distinctive almond shape. Her facial features were classically those of a Down Syndrome child. Leah was immediately reminded of her cousin Mary.

The girl studied Leah intently for a moment, taking in Leah's soft, fair, curling hair, which she'd pulled into an unruly twist, her heart-shaped face and sparkling green eyes, the slim figure beneath the dreadful uniform, the practical shoes. Then Ariana smiled. It was as though a light had come on. Every corner of the room seemed a little brighter, every color a little more brilliant. With surprising grace she stood and moved toward Leah, her fingers outstretched. "Are you going to be my new friend?"

"I'd like that very much." Leah meant it with her whole heart. She was also very aware of her employer's scrutiny.

"Can you play games? Checkers?" Other than a slight hesitation between her words, Ariana's pronunciation was distinct and clear. "I play the piano, too," Ariana announced cheerfully, then her lips turned downward. "But I make funny sounds."

"Perhaps we could learn some songs together."

"Teach me now!" Leah allowed herself to be led over to the piano. However, as they passed the open French doors, Ariana's attention was drawn to the garden. "See my flowers?" As Ariana gazed through the tiny windowpanes at the lush floral pathwork, Leah studied her.

The girl was well cared for. Her hair gleamed like polished gold, and her clothes fitted to perfection, although they were apparently chosen by someone not acquainted with current fashion trends. Ariana's nails were manicured and buffed to a soft sheen. She was obviously happy. The flowers had brought a smile to her lips. When her brother walked over and rested his hands on her shoulders, the smile deepened. Leah could sense the love flowing between the two of them as Adams's sensual lips and well-shaped jaw relaxed.

"It's time for your afternoon snack, Ariana," Mrs. Bright called from the doorway. Ariana glanced wistfully at Leah before disappearing into the kitchen with the rotund Mrs. Bright.

"Is your car open?" Leah was startled to find Marc Adams standing so near, and she barely managed to nod. "Then I'll carry your bags inside." He examined her with blatant interest. "I don't mean to be rude, but I hope by dinnertime you'll have disposed of that uniform. Surely your agency approves of something more attractive. Don't be offended, Ms. Brock,'' he added as he strode to the door. "I simply think it borders on the criminal to cover such assets with a thing that looks like a gunnysack.''

Hiding an amused and satisfied smile, Leah leisurely walked to a brocade couch and sat down, scanning the list she'd been given. "Ariana's schedule'' was a precise detailed listing, quarter hour by quarter hour, of the girl's day—her meals, her rest periods, even a time for "educational toys and games.'' Leah had never seen anything quite like it. Ariana's entire life was laid out on this page. There was only one thing missing. A time for fun.

Leah had grown up in a spontaneous unstructured household, completely different from the military discipline with which this household was obviously run. No wonder Ariana was so eager to pluck out a few tunes on the piano. Any diversion would do! It was difficult for Leah to imagine a childhood in this big silent place.

"Ms. Brock?'' Mrs. Bright stood in the doorway twisting her hands nervously. "Mr. Marc has taken your bags upstairs. He had to make a phone call. Ariana is watching a program on television. Perhaps it would be a good time to show you to your room. Mr. Marc doesn't like Ariana to be left alone for very long.''

Leah glanced at the schedule. There it was—"3:00-3:30—supervised television.''

Leah followed the woman up the curving staircase to the elegant second floor. The colors here were pastel, pale peaches and greens, an occasional touch of pink. Leah's own room was feminine and gracious, decorated in ivory with touches of mint green and perfectly suited to her taste. "How beautiful!'' Leah turned to the housekeeper, her eyes sparkling in delight. "I wish my roommate, Christina, could see this. She's alone in the apartment now that I've taken the job here. She'd be jealous, I'm sure. This is absolutely lovely.''

"It is, isn't it? Mrs. Adams had the house redone four years ago, just before..." Mrs. Bright seemed unable to continue. "Oh, my."

"It must have been a very great tragedy," Leah said sympathetically.

"I thought Mr. Marc was going to lose his mind with grief and worry. He was working day and night to get his practice established. Suddenly his parents were gone and he had Ariana to care for...." Mrs. Bright shook her head mournfully as she placed a suitcase on a nearby stand. "Fortunately his mother was always very definite about Ariana's care. He's had no decisions to make there. Dr. Carmichael has been Ariana's physician since her birth and has been very helpful. We've done our best to raise her as her parents might have."

Mrs. Bright was obviously off and running on one of her favorite subjects. "Mr. Marc's a miracle, if you ask me. Smart as a whip. Did you notice the brass rubbings downstairs? Did them himself in college. He traveled all over Europe. A bit of an archaeology buff, he is. And a sportsman, too! He's a horseman—or at least he was. Haven't heard much of it these past few years."

The words of praise bubbled from Mrs. Bright. "He's the kind of man any woman might want for a son. His mother would have been proud of him. A perfect gentleman. Very organized, of course, and meticulous." She clucked like a mother hen. "He has to be, considering all he does."

"I suppose," Leah agreed dubiously. Who'd ever heard of anything so ridiculous as "supervised television" for a seventeen-year-old? If she didn't do anything else for Ariana, she'd show her a little plain, old-fashioned, unorganized, laugh-till-your-sides-hurt fun—the kind she'd grown up thinking every family enjoyed.

"I'd better get back to Ariana," Mrs. Bright said. "Take your time unpacking. Mr. Marc is in his study. He'll go over your duties with you later."

He'd stayed home to observe her, Leah realized with a start, feeling more than ever like a bug beneath a microscope. The man had every right to spend the afternoon in his own home. What disturbed Leah was her intuitive sense that he'd be opposed to her approach to Ariana's care.

"I'll be in the kitchen if you need me." Mrs. Bright went downstairs, leaving Leah to explore her room.

Leah kicked off the sturdy regulation shoes the agency had recommended and curled her toes into the thick woolly carpet. She opened the doors to a large walk-in closet that was almost bigger than her bedroom at the apartment. She tested the bed with a few tentative bounces before stretching out full-length. "If all nannies got rooms like this, my agency would thrive from day one," she murmured blissfully.

Although there was a great need for a service that catered to families of special-needs children, finding qualified nannies—teachers, nurses or those specially trained to deal with the handicapped—was, not unexpectedly, a difficult task. Fortunately Leah already had a recruitment campaign mapped out. Other considerations, such as office space, an answering service, even the first round of advertising for the "Nonesuch Nannies" were all arranged.

She had discovered an ideal business location in a building that housed the offices of several pediatricians and children's dentists. Her space demands were low and the high visibility the spot afforded was perfect. Her future office, once a janitor's supply closet and storage room, would be remodeled to have a windowed front as part of her lease arrangement.

The owners of the building had put her relatively minor renovation low on their priority list, however, which was fine with Leah. Until she had some genuine job experience herself, she was in no hurry to begin interviewing applicants.

As Leah got up to unpack her suitcase, she remembered Marc Adams's dislike of her prescribed uniform. She gratefully unbuttoned it, letting it fall in a puddle around her slim ankles. If dowdy gray wasn't appropriate for a nanny, what was? She thought longingly of her well-worn blue jeans and oversize sweatshirt before deciding on a pale peach blouse and floral skirt.

She leisurely put away her few clothes, then found her way downstairs. Peeking into the TV room, she saw Ariana raptly watching an educational video. Mrs. Bright hovered in the kitchen, one eye on Ariana, the other on the cake she was frosting.

As she passed the study, Leah glanced in. Marc Adams sat at his desk, backed by floor-to-ceiling bookshelves. He'd discarded his jacket and rolled up his sleeves to reveal muscular forearms covered with soft dark hair. The unruly lock had fallen over one eye and he'd stuck a pencil behind his ear. He seemed very much in his element in this warm private room with its leather-bound books and burgundy draperies. As he looked up from his papers and smiled, Leah hurried into the kitchen.

"Done already? That didn't take long." With a thrust of her spatula, Mrs. Bright gestured to the stool across the counter from her.

"I didn't bring many clothes. The agency led me to believe I'd be wearing uniforms."

Mrs. Bright chuckled. "Mr. Marc didn't like that one bit, I'll wager. Besides, you're too pretty to hide under gray sackcloth."

"It *is* a depressing outfit. By the way, does Ariana own any play clothes? Blue jeans, that sort of thing?"

"Whatever for? When would she use them? There're supervised games, but she really doesn't *play*—not like a tiny child might."

"What about for picnics and walks in the park?"

"Her mother always insisted she look as nice as she could," Mrs. Bright said stubbornly. "That didn't include blue jeans."

"And Mr. Adams just picked up where his mother left off?"

"He didn't have much choice. He was already at Harvard when Ariana was born. He got his juris doctorate and his juris masters before he began to practice law. He and Ariana never spent more than an occasional holiday together until . . ." Mrs. Bright gestured in dismay.

"All I can say is I'm glad you're here. Ariana needs more than just me around this huge old house. I love her dearly—" she shook her head "—I'm not as young as I used to be. And Mr. Marc is just so busy. He's trying to do things exactly the way his parents did. . . ." She faltered guiltily. "I really shouldn't be talking. Ariana is the most well-cared-for child I've ever seen."

"A little too well cared for?" Leah asked softly. "Too regimented?"

Mrs. Bright's features relaxed. "You see it already, then?"

Leah patted the pocket of her skirt. "I have her schedule right here. And her list of doctors, dentists and nutritionists."

"That was set up by Mrs. Adams before she died. And Mr. Marc follows it to the letter." Mrs. Brock swirled one last bit of frosting onto the cake and placed it under a crystal cover. "I've worked here since Ariana was five. All this time, they've treated that child like a hothouse flower instead of a sturdy little daisy who could use real sunshine and rain."

Leah cupped her chin in her hands and stared levelly at the housekeeper. "Ariana's birth was a surprise?"

"You can say that again!" Mrs. Bright sputtered.

"Older parents are often more nervous and fearful than younger ones," Leah observed.

Mrs. Bright glanced in Ariana's direction. "And Mr. Marc, who's never had children, has only his own parents as examples of how to raise a child. Don't get me wrong—" Mrs. Bright's face flushed pink "—he's a fine man. The best. I wouldn't want you to think I'm disloyal."

Leah remembered Marc Adams had said he was divorced. What had gone wrong? Had children been an issue? She touched Mrs. Bright's arm, wishing she dared to ask more. "Thank you for telling me."

"Mrs. Bright, where's...?" Marc pushed through the swinging door into the kitchen. "Oh, excuse me," he said. A ringing timer shattered the ensuing silence.

"Ariana has free time on the patio right now," Mrs. Bright announced.

"Why don't I take her?" Leah offered, silently wondering how *free* time could be when one was told where to spend it.

Marc's heavy footsteps sounded behind her, making her stiffen. She turned to look warily over her shoulder. "Don't you trust me, Mr. Adams?"

"I'm not sure yet, Ms. Brock," he answered. "And perhaps we should make it Marc and Leah."

Ariana met them in the doorway. "Can you teach me to play the piano now?"

"I can. Or would you like to show me the flowers?"

The girl considered her important decision. "The flowers. We can play the piano when it rains." As Ariana showed her brother and Leah through the flower beds, calling out the blooms by name, more and more questions about Marc Adams formed in Leah's mind.

How did he feel about the responsibility he'd inherited? Why did he feel it necessary to live such a regimented and unyielding life? And what about women—was there someone special in his life now?

Abruptly Leah realized that she'd been murmuring a polite "mmm" to Ariana's chatter while her mind focused on

Marc. That had to stop. Ariana was the all-important one here.

Ariana tucked her hand into the crook of Leah's arm, talking animatedly, occasionally reaching out to touch one of Leah's soft blond waves. Unexpectedly she declared, "I'd like curls like yours."

"But you have beautiful hair, Ariana. It shines like gold."

"It's straight as sticks. Mrs. Bright says so." Ariana started to pout.

"Well, maybe someday we could fix your hair...."

Marc looked disapproving. "There's really no need for Ariana to be fussing with her hair."

"All teenage girls do," Leah pointed out matter-of-factly, giving him a reassuring smile. "We'll have a little fun. Nothing radical."

"I hope not." He appeared oddly uncomfortable, almost ill at ease. "If you'll excuse me now, I'll go back to my study."

"Why don't we make a list of things you want to do, like play the piano and have your hair done?" Leah suggested when Marc had gone. "Every day we'll pick one fun thing to do, starting tomorrow."

When they returned to the house, Mrs. Bright bustled onto the porch. "Dinner will be served in a few minutes. Mr. Marc would like to see you first, Leah." Ariana took Mrs. Bright's hand and allowed herself to be led into the kitchen.

On the way to the study, Leah smoothed the front of her skirt with her palms, wondering if this outfit was acceptable. As she knocked at the study door, Leah realized that she was hoping *everything* about her was acceptable to Marc. Including things that had nothing to do with her new job...

CHAPTER TWO

MARC WAS STARING out the French doors at the gardens. He'd removed his jacket, revealing a lean, muscular body; his hair was tousled, as if he'd been running his fingers through the dark strands. He turned as Leah entered, and gestured toward the couch.

She sank into its richly upholstered comfort, while he took the chair across from her. He straightened the sharp pleat of his trousers and studied her from beneath dark lashes.

"I suppose I should explain the comment I made earlier today concerning your uniform. It's just that you looked so much more... appealing, uh, attractive...."

Leah gave him a satisfied little smile. "It's all right. I didn't like it, either."

Marc's teeth were even and white, his lips soft and inviting as he smiled back. "Good. I was afraid I'd offended you."

"It takes more than that." Leah heard her pulse hammering in her ears and felt her palms grow damp as he studied her with undisguised interest.

"Most evenings, Ariana and I dine alone. Since you'll be Ariana's primary caretaker, I think it would be best if, instead of eating in the kitchen, you joined us. Would you mind?"

"Not at all! It will give Ariana and me a chance to tell you about what we've done."

"You'll have Sundays off. I've already made plans to spend that day with her, and I don't like tampering with her schedule."

Of course he didn't! Leah thought wryly. He probably had everything planned for the rest of Ariana's life and his own—right down to the socks he'd wear a week from Tuesday. Curiosity finally got the best of her. "Does Ariana ever leave the house?" she asked cautiously.

Adams stared at Leah as if he didn't quite comprehend her question. "Leave? Why?"

"For a change of pace. *You* get out every day. Shouldn't Ariana have the same opportunity?" Though disapproval seemed to radiate from him in waves, Leah persisted. "Keeping people like Ariana at home behind closed doors is a thing of the past. According to some of my professors—"

"What's good for me and what's good for her are two entirely different matters," he interrupted coldly.

"Not really." Leah momentarily forgot her manners in her quest to make a point. "You both need friends!"

"Ariana has Mrs. Bright." His dark eyes narrowed. "And now, for better or worse, she has you."

Leah quickly interpreted his message. *Your theories and studies do not influence me. Ariana is different from the rest of us. Ariana does not go out.*

"I'm sorry," Leah apologized. "I was out of line. Sometimes I get carried away."

"You *were* out of line." A tight smile flickered across his face. "But you're forgiven. My sister needs a champion like you."

"Then you don't mind if I plan some outings for her?" Leah asked eagerly.

"I didn't say that." The black look stole back into his expression. "Ariana is not accustomed to being in the public eye. I don't want her upset, frightened or ridiculed in any way. Ariana is a...challenged child. She doesn't need any more obstacles to overcome. I prefer that she stay here where she's comfortable and safe.''

"Your sister is retarded and you don't want her to leave the house, is that it?"

Marc recoiled and started to speak.

Leah ignored him. "I realize that the word 'retarded' may be out of vogue, but I don't believe in euphemisms. We all have to be very clearheaded about your sister in order to help her live up to her potential, don't you think?" After a long moment of awkward silence, Leah continued. "Did she leave the house when your parents were alive?"

"Never. Everything Ariana needs is brought here. She leaves only to visit the dentist. Even that is very upsetting."

"Of course," Leah said. "Trips to the dentist are distressing for me, too, but that doesn't keep me trapped in the house all day."

"I don't care to discuss this further." He rose impatiently. "You may understand the handicapped in theory, but you're short on experience."

"My cousin Mary—"

"—is obviously of a different temperament than Ariana. I know my sister. Learn the rules of the house, Ms. Brock. As long as you understand what I expect of you, everything will be fine."

There was no arguing with that tone. Marc Adams was the most incredibly handsome stuffed shirt she'd ever seen. But she wasn't giving up hope. She'd just have to use other tactics to bring some spontaneity into Ariana's life. Leah was already plotting her strategy when she felt his hand on her elbow. As his thumb grazed her skin, her thoughts went skittering off in a thousand different directions.

ARIANA WAS ALREADY seated at the table when they entered the dining room. Wearing a pretty silk blouse that made her blue eyes sparkle, she sat patiently with her hands folded in her lap. Leah might not agree with all of Marc's theories, but she had to admit that he'd helped raise a charming girl.

"I'm hungry, Marc," Ariana announced plaintively.

Marc smiled at his sister as he drew out Leah's chair. As Leah slipped into the seat, her arm brushed the sleeve of his coat, allowing her to feel the warmth and strength of his arm. The scent of his after-shave teased her nostrils. Grimly she planted herself in the chair and ignored the sparks of attraction racing through her system.

"Apple juice, my lady?" he asked Ariana with a flourish. He held a decanter of golden liquid over her glass. "It's made from the finest apples, fermented until just the right moment, then captured in high-quality aluminum...."

"Marc's teasing," Ariana explained to Leah with a delighted giggle.

"And you, Lady Brock. May I offer you some of this nectar from the gods?" Marc settled the juice decanter on the table and picked up a bottle of wine. Leah was intrigued by the dancing lights in his dark eyes. She lifted her glass to play along.

"It's my heart's desire, kind sir."

She was rewarded with a fleeting look that managed to be both playful and sensual, as he poured wine into her goblet.

"Surely your heart desires something a little more significant than a simple Chardonnay," he murmured.

Leah couldn't think of anything else to say.

By the time the layer cake was served, the atmosphere around the table was festive. Ariana clapped her hands and chortled, "This is fun, Marc! Let's have a party every night!"

A frown settled between his eyes. "Ariana, you may go upstairs with Mrs. Bright," he instructed. "I'd like to visit with Leah alone."

Ariana gazed longingly at Leah as if she were a shiny trinket just out of reach. Then she sighed, pushed away from the table and went into the kitchen.

When she'd gone, Marc rose to help Leah from her chair. "We'll talk in the living room," he said abruptly. ":It's more . . . comfortable there."

Once in the other room, he settled himself in an over-stuffed armchair and laced his fingers together, watching her closely. "You're already wondering what you're doing here—in this house of rules and regulations—aren't you?"

"I'm sorry you think that. My inexperience must be showing," Leah said, feigning lightheartedness.

"Your enthusiasm, more likely."

Leah couldn't meet his gaze. "I'd hope that was an asset, not a liability."

"As long as you stay within the boundaries I set for you, it is. I trust the life-style my parents created for Ariana. She shouldn't be exposed to outside elements that might upset her."

"People staring, for instance?" Leah asked bluntly.

Marc flinched, obviously hurt by a memory. "It pained my mother a great deal to think of thoughtless people staring at her daughter. Or worse yet, laughing at her."

"Ariana is lovely, vivacious and thoroughly delightful. Have you considered that people might *like* her?"

He looked at her pityingly. "You're very naive, aren't you, Leah?"

"Not everyone sees the handicapped as the butt of jokes," Leah muttered. "Everything I've studied tells me that Ariana deserves the opportunity to enjoy a full life."

"She has one here." His voice was flat, unrelenting.

"But there's life outside this house!"

"Not for Ariana." As Marc stood and towered over her, Leah shrank back, regretting the passion she felt for this isolated innocent child.

He paced from his chair to the French doors and back again. "I expect you to follow Ariana's schedule to the letter. I've consulted several experts about the system we use in this household. If something appears to be awry, consult me. Mrs. Bright will be in charge of her meals and her eating schedule. However, Ariana does need some new clothes. If you'd like to shop for them, it would save us time and trouble."

"I'd love to!"

Some of his frostiness subsided. "Good. Mrs. Bright can tell you what she needs. Perhaps you could take care of it tomorrow." A shadow of doubt crossed his face as he added, "Surely nothing can go wrong during one little shopping expedition."

She ignored the warning in his look and plunged ahead. "Marc, there's something else. I'd like to see time in Ariana's schedule for play."

Marc's impatience was apparent. "I believe that's 'educational games and puzzles.'"

"But what about *fun?*" She leaned forward urgently. "Picnics on the grass! Swimming! Listening to rock music! Dancing!"

His frown was so deep and dark that it startled her. "Do you know what you're asking?"

"Yes. Ariana is seventeen. Even though she's retarded, there's no reason she can't keep up with the rest of the world." An idea struck her. "Besides, dancing is healthy exercise."

Marc scowled. "I don't think my mother would have approved."

"Marvelous exercise, in fact. It's excellent for coordination. If she's not interested, I'll drop the subject immediately."

"I'm not sure what fun has to do with any of this, Leah."

"Don't you ever have fun?" She regretted the question the moment she asked it.

"I haven't had much fun in the past four years, if that's what you mean." His voice was bleak. "Ariana's been the only bright spot in an otherwise stressful existence. My parents' deaths, establishing the law practice, maintaining the house... Of course it hasn't always been fun!"

"I'm sorry. I didn't mean to bring up painful memories." Leah drooped in her chair. "I think I need a muzzle."

Startled, he threw back his head and laughed. The strong cords and muscles in his neck played beneath the tanned skin, and his eyes, usually so dark and serious, twinkled. "You might at that, but maybe a breath of fresh air is what this old house needs right now." In his expression Leah saw a combination of pure male interest and cautious warning. "As long as you follow the rules."

Like quicksilver his attitude had sobered. "My mother always worried about what would become of Ariana when she and my father were gone. That circumstance was inevitable, of course, but she didn't foresee it happening so soon. Almost monthly I received a letter from either her or my father reminding me of my 'responsibility.' In fact, the day I saw them off, on their way to Scotland, they made me swear that if anything happened to them I'd continue to raise Ariana just as they had." He stared blankly at the unlit fireplace.

It was a heavy burden and an unfair one, Leah thought. Ariana's parents had created an artificial world for their daughter and extracted a promise from Marc to keep the world intact. No wonder he was so grim.

Leah made another mental note. Marc Adams needed a little fun in his life, too. Could she achieve that?

MARC HAD ALREADY LEFT for work when Leah came downstairs the next morning. Ariana was helping Mrs. Bright cut cookies from the dough the older woman was rolling on the kitchen counter.

"Look, Leah, gingerbread people!"

"Yum." Leah helped herself to coffee and settled on a stool near Ariana. "I didn't know you could bake."

"Can't. Marc says I mustn't touch the stove. But I'm a good cookie cutter!" Ariana was neatly dressed in a white short-sleeved shirt and a navy pleated skirt. Her shoes were solid, sensible penny loafers. As usual, her hair was brushed to a gloss and hanging down her back. All she needed to look like a schoolgirl in uniform was a stiff navy blazer with an emblem on the pocket and a book bag over one arm.

"Ariana, have you ever gone to school?" Leah wondered.

It was Mrs. Bright who answered. "She has a tutor during the winter months. She could go to the public school's special-education classes if Mr. Marc approved. As it is, she has her classes in a bedroom we've made into a schoolroom. He said he'd appreciate your help over the summer. If Ariana doesn't practice what she's learned—printing and the like—she tends to forget."

"We can have fun with that, can't we, Ariana?" Leah was happy to help in any way she could. "You'll have to show me what words you know."

Marc had certainly insulated the girl from any and every incident that might cause her stress, Leah mused. Surely he realized that he wouldn't always be available to protect Ariana.

"Ariana," Leah said, "your brother told me I could get you some new clothes today."

"Can I come, too?" Ariana asked hopefully.

Mrs. Bright stared at Ariana in amazement. "You've never gone shopping!"

After Marc's terse admonishment to Leah that she follow his rules and regulations, she knew it was impossible to take the girl with her. "I'll do it as quickly as I can. And I'll bring lots of selections."

"Oh, she doesn't get choices," Mrs. Bright announced as she pulled yet another list from a drawer. "These are sizes, brand names and stores. Just bring what she needs." The housekeeper tucked the list and a wad of bills into Leah's hand.

She *needs* choices, Leah thought stubbornly as she folded the money and stuffed it into her pocket. Didn't anyone give Ariana credit for having her own opinions? Marc and his family had made Ariana a lavish cocoon. Couldn't he see that she had no chance of becoming a butterfly if she wasn't allowed to leave it?

ARIANA WAS WAITING at the door when Leah returned from the mall. Leah felt a quick stab of guilt for avoiding the staid department stores Mrs. Bright had recommended. Still, she'd tried to be responsible. Over a cup of espresso she'd deliberated long and hard about calling Dr. Carmichael. When she finally did, they had a long talk and, with his approval, she'd added several rhythmic "golden oldie" tapes and an exercise video to her purchases.

"Did you buy me things?" Ariana asked breathlessly. "Lots?"

"Mr. Marc won't like it" was Mrs. Bright's gloomy prediction, as she eyed the mound of packages.

Leah's confidence wavered and she remembered the look of warning he'd given her when he'd suggested she buy the clothes. Though the shopping spree would probably throw her into further discord with Marc, it was too late for regrets now. Ariana was already kneeling on the kitchen floor digging through the parcels.

"Look! It sparkles!" Ariana clutched a rhinestone-and-sequin-studded sweatshirt to her cheek.

Leah knelt beside her. "I picked one with a flower on it for you, Ariana, because I know you love them."

"Those spangles aren't going to be easy to wash. And where's the child going to wear that thing, anyway?"

Mrs. Bright's words put even more doubts into Leah's mind, but she pushed those thoughts away. "It's a sweat-shirt. She can wear it around the house. And if we're careful, we can hand-wash it."

"Hmph!" snorted Mrs. Bright as she slammed her kettles around loudly.

Leah judiciously hustled the excited girl to her bedroom, away from Mrs. Bright's stolid practicality. There, Ariana went joyfully from package to package, insisting every piece of clothing was more wonderful than the last. Leah had rejected navy and white for a rainbow of colors—teals and greens, red and oranges, pinks and blues. The sweatshirt and a pair of blue jeans were Ariana's favorite items.

"Can I wear these?" she asked, awe in her voice. "Really?"

"After your afternoon exercise."

"I don't want to walk in the garden today." Ariana ran her fingers across the shiny front of her sequined top. "I want to wear this."

"I bought you a warm-up suit."

"I'm already warm."

"No, honey, it's for exercising." Leah pulled a pair of pale blue sweatpants out of a shopping bag.

"Funny," Ariana giggled. "Marc wears those to go jogging."

"Exactly. Now you can exercise just like Marc."

"I can't jog."

"No, but you can do this," Leah said, producing her pièce de résistance. "It's an exercise tape. I called Dr. Carmichael and he said you could use it." Leah coaxed the curious girl into the family room and popped the video into the VCR. A young woman in a skimpy leotard flashed onto the screen.

Ariana started to imitate the woman on the tape. When she couldn't keep up, she simply fanned her arms in the air and chortled. Leah urged Ariana to put on her new sweatpants, while she herself changed into a pair of brief nylon shorts and a body-hugging T-shirt.

"We're going to do a little more stretching now," the taped voice confided. "Bend at the waist, grab your ankles and hold for a really big stretch. If you can't reach your ankles, touch your knees or your thighs...."

Leah, who was naturally limber, closed her eyes, folded nimbly in half and breathed deeply. Still upside down, she glanced through her wide-spread knees to see an astounded Marc Adams standing in the doorway.

"Look, Marc, I'm exercising!" Ariana flapped her hands vigorously. "And I'm wearing funny pants like you!"

Leah could tell that Marc was struggling to maintain his composure. His dark eyes were wide and he was scowling openly. With a sinking sensation in her stomach, she righted herself, tugging at the hem of her too-short shorts. Mentally she began packing her bags for the trip back to her apartment.

"What is the meaning of this?" He hovered over them, apparently torn between shock and—could it be?—amusement.

"Exercise time," Leah explained timidly. "It's on the schedule."

"I mean, what is the meaning of *this?*" He pointed a blunt, finely shaped fingernail at Ariana's baggy sweats and the still-bouncing image on the TV screen.

"I thought it might be nice if Ariana could vary her routine. I called her doctor from the mall and okayed it with him. In fact, Dr. Carmichael recommended two other tapes we might try. I was thinking—"

"You seem to be thinking all the time," Marc interrupted. "Perhaps you should do a little less of it during your stay here. I've worked out a routine for my sister, and I don't want it disrupted again." His gaze drifted to the endearing sight of Ariana, her face shining, dancing happily about the room. "She's not used to this. Don't let her overdo it."

"We'll warm up and cool down faithfully." Leah's heart thumped double time to a strange rumba beat that had more to do with Marc's presence than her exertion.

"If there are any problems, this comes to a halt immediately. And," he added sternly, "I intend to talk to Dr. Carmichael myself."

With a start, Leah realized that Marc's expression of wary resignation had been replaced by a look of disguised admiration. She pulled at the hem of her shorts in a vain effort to cover her thighs.

Reluctantly he tore his eyes from her softly rounded hips and retreated toward the door. "I, uh, came to pick up an unfinished brief that I left in the study. I'd better get back to the office." He gave Leah one last look. "I hope that dinner tonight offers no additional surprises, Ms. Brock."

"Watch me, Leah!" Ariana squealed, making awkward little jumps across the Persian carpet, her face aglow. Pleased, Leah dropped onto the nearest couch to enjoy the performance. She'd injected plenty of new life into Ariana's existence—enough for one day.

WHILE ARIANA BATHED, Leah folded the controversial clothes in a pile at the foot of the bed and laid out a dark brown skirt and pale ivory blouse for the girl to wear to dinner.

Ariana came into the room wrapped in a fuzzy white robe, her hair damp and clinging to her cheeks. She reached to touch Leah's springy curls. "Your hair is pretty."

"Ariana, would you like me to do your hair for dinner?"

"Like yours?" Ariana shook her head so forcefully, droplets of water sprayed across the room.

"Not exactly. I've got natural curl in mine. But I do have a banana clip in my room we could use."

"Don't want bananas in my hair!"

Leah smiled indulgently as she led Ariana into the room. "Come on, I'll show you what I mean."

"Will Marc like it?" Ariana wondered some minutes later. Her hair was drawn away from her face and cascaded dramatically over one shoulder.

"I hope so," Leah murmured as she watched Ariana primp in front of the mirror. "Otherwise I might be in trouble—again."

While Ariana changed, Leah showered and slipped into a sundress. Though the back was low, the bodice was quite decorous. She'd pulled her own hair into a French twist and put on a touch of makeup, hoping she'd pass for a proper nanny.

"Ready for dinner?" Leah called out as she knocked on Ariana's door.

"I can come down by myself," the girl insisted.

Already she was taking more responsibility for herself! Those dreadful lists of Marc's had prevented Ariana from learning to make decisions, and Leah was delighted that was so willing to attempt new things without assistance. Happily Leah meandered downstairs.

"Is Ariana with you?" Marc called from the study.

"She wanted to come down alone."

Though his eyebrow arched in surprise, he made no comment as he gestured her to enter.

"Ariana loves the exercise tape," she ventured shyly, engulfed by the room's scent of after-shave, leather and wood. "I know she'll use it often."

"You're intimating that Ariana should be making choices for herself," he said, tilting backward in his chair. "Our mother would have been shocked by the display I saw today."

He'd been more than a little shocked himself, Leah thought slyly, remembering his expression as he'd taken in her bare legs. She had the satisfying notion that he was nearly as attracted to her as she was to him. He looked particularly appealing tonight in dark casual trousers and a black turtleneck sweater that showcased the impressive bulge of his biceps.

"In fact," he continued, "I've invited Dr. Carmichael to dinner. It might be helpful for the two of you to meet. Mother always trusted Dr. Carmichael's opinions. He's been Ariana's pediatrician since her birth. Besides, it's been a long time since we've had guests."

"Does he approve of the strict schedule you keep?"

"He's aware that Mother devised it and I've adhered to it."

"But maybe Mother wasn't always right." Leah wanted to take back the words even as she spoke.

Adams gave her a cool appraising stare. "You're overstepping your bounds, Ms. Brock." He tapped his fingers on the desk blotter and quirked one eyebrow. "If that agency had issued a storm warning, I might have been more prepared for you, Leah."

"I don't know what's come over me. I'm not usually so rude." She sighed. "Or willful. Or thoughtless."

A tight smile softened his features. "No more changes without permission?"

"I'll try, but what about the tape? Ariana loves it."

"If I hadn't seen it for myself, I wouldn't have believed it."

"Ariana is a darling girl, but she's much too sheltered. There are so many things she'd enjoy. I'd love to take her to the theater. It's one of my favorite forms of entertainment. If only—"

Marc spoke with exaggerated patience, repeating what she'd already heard. "Leah, when my parents died and I became my sister's guardian, I decided to care for her just as they had. It was what they wanted. They were fine people. Loving people. I don't want someone second-guessing my decisions now. It wasn't easy for me to set up housekeeping for Ariana, but I've done my best. I want you to believe that."

"I don't doubt it. It's just that Ariana is a teenager."

"She's retarded."

"But a teenager nevertheless. Shouldn't she have the opportunity to enjoy a few of the things other teens do?"

Emotions moved like shadows across Marc's face. "This conversation is over, Leah. You know my wishes. We'll follow the guidelines my parents set."

At that moment the doorbell rang. "It appears Dr. Carmichael has arrived," Marc said briskly, taking Leah by the elbow and guiding her toward the door. She relished the strength of his fingers and the sureness of his step as they moved to meet the doctor.

Dr. Carmichael was in his early sixties, a rotund cheerful man with a brisk no-nonsense manner. Leah liked him immediately. They were still chatting in the hallway when Mrs. Bright announced dinner. "Ariana's waiting, sir." Her voice cracked slightly.

"She must be very hungry," Dr. Carmichael commented.

"She's *something,* all right," Mrs. Bright muttered, giving little hint of what would greet them when they entered the dining room.

Marc strode in first. "Good evening, Ariana. I'm sorry we kept you wait—" His words ended in a strangled choke.

As Leah entered the room, a small utterance of dismay escaped her. *Not this, Ariana! Not tonight!*

The girl was standing at the bay window looking out at the garden. Her hair trailed out of the banana clip and over her shoulder, just as Leah had styled it. Instead of the prim-and-proper outfit Leah had planned for her, Ariana wore the bright glittery sweatshirt, which she'd paired with her brand-new blue jeans.

Marc's face flushed darkly. "What's going on?"

Behind Leah, Dr. Carmichael coughed.

"Do you like my outfit, Marc? Isn't it beautiful?" Ariana rubbed the sequined front. "*I'm* beautiful!"

So simple, so true. *I'm beautiful.* And obvious to all of them that, for the first time in her life, Ariana believed it.

"Marc, I—"

"Not now, Leah." He placed his hand on her arm and led her to the table.

During dinner, while Ariana preened like an exotic bird, Leah's attention careened from Ariana's delighted smile to Marc's grim expression. Dr. Carmichael spent most of the meal observing the situation with quiet but unmistakable interest.

"Mrs. Bright, would you see to Ariana tonight?" Marc asked when she came to clear the table. "Ms. Brock and I have several things to discuss." He glowered. "Again." His words were foreboding. "Doctor, would you join us?"

Dr. Carmichael shook his head emphatically as he glanced from Marc to Leah and back again, looking entirely too amused. "No, I don't think so. But I would like to talk to you for a moment first, Marc."

They left Leah alone to trail miserably into the living room. Fired. How was that going to sound? The prospective owner and manager of a nanny service fired by her first employer.

The room was warm and dusky, thanks to a small fire in the fireplace. Marc's after-shave still lingered in the air. Leah swallowed thickly. An assault on her character and reputation was quite enough; this delicious assault on her senses only added insult to injury.

"An after-dinner brandy, Ms. Brock?" He entered silently and, without waiting for an answer, poured an amber splash into each of two snifters.

Leah took the glass and with her free hand rubbed her bare arm, now covered with nervous gooseflesh.

Marc lowered himself into a wing chair and warmed the snifter between his hands. He was silent for a long time.

Leah could hear a clock ticking and the crackle of burning wood.

"What are you up to, Ms. Brock?" he asked suddenly.

Leah returned his steady gaze. "Up to? Nothing."

"I don't believe that. You've been here less than two days, and already you've managed to set this entire household on its ear. Disrupting schedules, changing Ariana's attitude and appearance, breaking rules . . ."

"I didn't realize I'd infiltrated a military operation when I came here, Mr. Adams. I thought I came to care for a handicapped child. It was my understanding that you *wanted* my input. I'm very well trained, and I consider myself highly qualified to work with the handicapped. My master's thesis concerns 'mainstreaming' handicapped children into regular schools. I have letters of recommendation from all my professors. If you didn't want someone who was going to be innovative, why did you hire me?"

"I've been wondering that myself," he muttered grimly, then swallowed his brandy. "You've created a significant disturbance in a household that's run smoothly for four years," Marc accused, his eyes distinctly troubled.

"But Ariana's happy."

"She was happy before."

"I believe she's happier now." Leah's words were soft but spoken with conviction.

Marc sighed and stared into his empty glass. "Perhaps you're right. Dr. Carmichael said as much in the hallway as he was leaving. If that thought hadn't crossed my mind, I would have fired you." He looked at her speculatively. "Ariana *was* different tonight. Almost like a . . . normal teenager."

"She needs joy in her life. We all do."

Marc's shoulders sagged. "Do we? I guess I've forgotten."

He seemed so vulnerable, so unguarded, that Leah's tender heart went out to him. "Let me work with Ariana.

Trust me to relieve some of your responsibilities," she pleaded. "Perhaps I can help bring some joy into your own life."

He didn't seem to hear. "Initially I thought you'd work out. Now..." He looked at her, baffled. "In the future please try to be more...conservative, Ms. Brock. This household can't tolerate radicals in any form. Even nannies."

"I'm sure Mrs. Bright could use my help," she murmured, hoping to escape before he changed his mind, "so if you'll excuse me..."

He stood just as she did. Accidentally their bodies brushed together thin cotton against worsted wool, softness against strength. Leah gave a little gasp of surprise. Even more astonishing was the quick brush of his lips across hers.

Before he could speak, Leah fled the room, her fingertips resting lightly where his touch still seared. All the way to the kitchen, she smiled.

CHAPTER THREE

"YOU AND MR. MARC haven't had words, have you?" Mrs. Bright asked Saturday morning, her round face creased with concern.

Leah manufactured an innocent expression before looking up from the paper. "A disagreement? Of course not."

Mrs. Bright punched the bread dough she was kneading. "I know it's none of my business, but the two of you haven't had much to say to each other this week. I just thought..."

"We're fine, Mrs. Bright. Just settling into a routine, that's all," Leah fibbed. *And trying to avoid one another ever since he kissed me.*

"Good. I wouldn't want anything to go wrong between the two of you. Ariana's been so happy this week."

To reassure Mrs. Bright—and herself—that her relationship with Marc had not soured over a simple kiss, Leah folded the paper and laid it aside. "Where is he, anyway?"

Leah followed the housekeeper's pointing finger to the vast entryway. The sun streamed through the open entrance and across the big peacock motif in the foyer, making it glimmer like a mosaic of precious stones. Beyond the doorway, Leah could see Marc, barefoot and shirtless, washing his ruby-red sports car.

She'd meant to remain in the shadowy cover of the house, but the tantalizing sight of bronzed muscles bunching and rippling across Marc's back as he worked enticed her into the sunlight.

"I'm gonna boogie till I drop, drop, drop! I'm gonna boogie without stop, stop, stop!" Ariana chanted at the top of her voice. "Boogie drop, boogie stop! Stop! Drop! Stop! Drop!" She bounced across the driveway in one direction and then another in happy abandon, dancing to the music emanating from the "boom box" positioned near the flower bed. "Come dance with me, Leah!"

Ever since Leah had introduced her to the exercise tape and fifties rock and roll, Ariana had spent her free time jiving, squirming, dancing or swaying to music. The disapproval in Marc's expression told Leah he wasn't completely convinced this was a good idea.

"In a minute, honey. I want to talk to your brother first. Do you think you could turn that music down a little?"

"Marc says it could wake the dead." Ariana peered around as if expecting a string of ghouls and mummies to stagger toward the house. "If I've already waked them, will they come here?"

Leah resisted a smile. "It's just a saying, Ariana. The only people you'll wake with your music are lazy ones like me." She turned to Marc. "Thank you for letting me sleep in. It felt wonderful."

"I thought we all needed a change of pace today." As Marc lifted the chamois in his hand, Leah noticed an appealing little dimple in his cheek. "If I hadn't become an attorney, I might have owned a chain of car washes. As a teenager, I perfected the art. I drove a vintage Thunderbird that I polished every time it left the garage."

"Marc, look at me!" Ariana cried. Leah gasped. Ariana had snatched up the garden hose and was splashing water across the newly waxed car. Water beaded on the red hood like sparkling diamonds and sprayed through an open window onto the leather interior. "I'm helping," she announced proudly, as all Marc's hard work vanished.

"You've helped enough now." Marc lifted the hose from her hand. "Why don't you let me take that before you get wet?"

Leah hurriedly picked up a dry cloth and began wiping the upholstery.

"You don't have to do that." His hand closed around her wrist and she felt the cool dampness of his skin. "It's only water."

"It's the least I can do. I'm the one who got to sleep in, remember?" Leah rubbed a little harder at the leather seat as Marc watched his sister bob and lunge on the driveway.

"She's quite graceful," Leah commented.

"My mother was a graceful woman. And musical. She had a brief career as a concert pianist." Marc bent to scrub too forcefully at a spot on the hood. "It never occurred to me that an interest like that was possible for my sister."

"Why not? Ariana is retarded, not deaf. Besides, even the deaf enjoy music if they can feel its rhythm." Leah stood back and regarded her work with a critical eye. "I think we missed a few spots over here...." As she reached across the hood, her arm grazed Marc's bare chest, sending a wave of physical longing through her body. Marc, obviously unaware of her response to him, hummed under his breath as he coaxed the shine back into his car.

Ariana continued her accompaniment. "Bop, bop, bop! Bop till you drop!"

"Who taught her that nonsense, anyway," Marc grumbled, looking directly at Leah. He leaned his hip harder against the fender and draped a muscular arm along the roof of the car.

"Guilty," Leah confessed. "She seems to like it."

"She'd probably like a kettle drum, too, but I'm not inclined to buy her one." His smile assured Leah that his grumpy words were just that—words.

She propped herself next to him. "Even *I* wouldn't recommend a kettle drum."

"Thank goodness for that."

"A small trap set, perhaps..."

He poked her with his knuckle. "Tease."

Every inadvertent brush of bare skin, every touch they shared, threw Leah's system into a state of alert. Could he feel it? Or was this compelling attraction entirely one-sided? As they wiped down the rest of the car, Leah was too aware of Marc to even trust herself to speak.

Ariana's singing finally forced Leah to break the silence. "Marc? Would it be all right for me to buy Ariana a toy microphone?"

Marc's lip curled slightly. "Are you planning on taking her on the road? A singing tour? Nightclub circuit?"

"A toy microphone will be adequate. You know, a pretend mike. I think she'd enjoy it.

His amazed look made her feel as if she'd just asked for two tickets on the space shuttle. "But why?"

Exasperated, Leah threw her hands in the air. "For fun, that's why! *I* don't need a reason to like music! It simply gives me pleasure. Ariana's no different."

"No, I suppose not," Marc conceded doubtfully. "It's just that my parents never—"

"They may have exposed her to more music if they'd thought she'd like it. Don't you think your mother would have loved knowing her daughter enjoyed music?"

"You should have been an attorney," Marc noted wryly. "A jury wouldn't stand a chance with you."

"Now, there's just one more little thing." Leah forged ahead, buoyed by her victory. "Ariana needs shorts. She'll be much more comfortable in them."

"No lady wears shorts." His words were prim and disapproving, clearly an echo from the past.

Leah stared at Marc. "What did you say?"

"I said, 'No lady wears shorts.' If I heard my mother say it once, I heard her say it a dozen times. My mother thought they were...vulgar."

"Do you?"

Marc's face turned pink beneath his tan. "Of course not. I like them."

"Then what's the problem?"

"It's my sister we're talking about. Mother would turn over in her grave if she knew Ariana was wearing shorts."

"But that's really not a problem, is it?" Leah persisted. "Your mother isn't here. Ariana's the one you should be considering."

"You're overstepping your position, Ms. Brock." His face darkened and his eyebrows met briefly over the bridge of his nose. Once again, Leah feared she'd gone too far. Then he relaxed. "One pair. No more. I'm not crazy about the idea, but if you want to see Ariana's reaction . . ."

"One pair of walking shorts. They'll be very discreet and . . . ladylike, I promise."

"Microphones and walking shorts." His voice held a note of wonder. "Next you'll be saying she needs a motorcycle and helmet."

Leah couldn't resist needling him. "There's no use giving her a motorcycle when she doesn't have her license."

Marc raised the wet chamois shoulder-high and was about to fling it at her when Mrs. Bright appeared in the doorway.

"Sir!" Mrs. Bright's startled yelp saved Leah.

"Ahem . . . yes, Mrs. Bright?" Marc made an obvious effort to regain a more dignified demeanor.

"I'm finished in the kitchen, sir. Dinner is all planned and ready for the oven. Since Leah . . . Miss Brock came, I've had so much more time that I'm caught up on my chores. I'll watch Ariana this afternoon, then Leah can get out of the house." Mrs. Bright hesitated. "You, too, Mr. Marc."

"That's very nice of you, Mrs. Bright," Leah began, "but I don't want to ask you to take over my duties. I can go out tomorrow—"

"I agree with Mrs. Bright," Marc interrupted, gesturing. "You should take a few hours off."

"Are you going to take her someplace, Marc?" Ariana asked as she wandered toward them.

"No. I didn't mean..."

"I think that's a fine idea, sir!" Mrs. Bright said agreeably. "If you and Miss Brock want to have dinner out, I'll put my dishes away. Ariana and I can have pancakes or soup for dinner."

"Take her, Marc." Unexpectedly Ariana grabbed Marc's hand and placed it over Leah's, which still rested on the hood of the car. She patted the entwined hands and announced with a beneficent smile, "I *love* pancakes."

They were frozen for a moment in an odd tableau, their hands linked, their eyes locked. Marc, clearly embarrassed, was the first to pull away. "To avoid further, uh, discussion, perhaps you'd like to see the new sculpture garden in my office complex, Ms. Brock. Mrs. Bright and Ariana seem determined to get rid of us."

"A—a quick look might be nice," she stammered. "We needn't stay away long—"

"Go now!" Ariana commanded.

Both Marc and Leah shot pleading looks at Mrs. Bright, but found no help in that quarter. The woman nodded with satisfaction. "Good. You both need a break. Ariana and I are going to have a wonderful day, aren't we, honey?"

"And pancakes."

Marc shrugged helplessly, apparently as befuddled as Leah by this surprising turn of events. "I think we've been kicked out of the house."

"It certainly seems that way."

"I suppose I should change clothes." He looked down at his bare chest. "Or at least put some on."

Leah returned to her bedroom in a daze. Whatever had possessed Ariana to start playing matchmaker?

She was still puzzling over it when Ariana waved good-bye from the front porch of the house. Leah leaned her head against the seat and closed her eyes. The interior of the car smelled pleasantly of leather and car wax. "I feel rather silly about this," she began.

"How do you think I feel?" The wind through the open window tugged at Marc's hair, blowing it away from his face to reveal a high chiseled forehead. His jaw was strong and resolute, his dark eyes alert. As he drove, Leah could almost see the tension seeping from his face. "The women in my household have become excessively bossy."

"They sure ganged up on us," Leah remarked. "I don't think that little scene was as spur of the moment as it seemed." She looked happily at the passing scenery. "However, I'm not altogether sorry they did this. It's a lovely afternoon."

"Since Mrs. Bright and Ariana have planned the day without us, we may as well enjoy it."

The sculpture garden was a lush, well-planned maze of shrubbery and flowers, with winding paths that led to pieces of impressive statuary. Twice, Marc and Leah became lost in the maze. The second time, Leah sighed exaggeratedly, batting at an overhanging branch. "This garden is in *your* office complex. Don't you know the way out?"

"I've never taken the time to look at it. Between the business and Ariana I just...forgot." Marc tipped his head back to view the sky. "It's nice, isn't it? It's been a long time since I've done anything for...fun." His expression was regretful, as if for the first time he realized he'd lost something important.

"Then Mrs. Bright had a good idea," Leah pointed out matter-of-factly. "You *did* need a change of pace."

Silently they returned to the car. Without comment Marc drove to a well-known Mexican restaurant. The stubborn set of his jaw as he guided her into the building told Leah that he was only doing this for Ariana.

While they waited at a table in the bar, Leah began to feel more and more miserable. Marc was blatantly unhappy about being saddled with his sister's nanny for the afternoon. It was apparent in the abrupt manner of his speech and the uneasy way his gaze shifted around the room. He was no doubt hoping to avoid meeting anyone he knew. Leah felt like an unwieldy piece of baggage—too large to stuff under the table and too valuable to leave behind.

She was relieved when their beverages and a basket of warm tortilla chips arrived, giving her something to do other than nervously clasp her hands. They ate and drank without exchanging a word. A warm lassitude flowed through her as the tequila in her margarita started to take effect.

The hostess led them to an isolated corner table, which had a horseshoe-shaped upholstered bench wrapped around it. A table for lovers, Leah thought. Her shoulder brushed Marc's as he slid in next to her. After the waitress filled their water glasses and handed them menus, she tugged at the thick velvet curtains that surrounded the booth, enclosing Leah and Marc in the intimate little space.

Leah shifted uncomfortably in her seat. But fortunately the dimness, the privacy of the booth and the drink began to have a bewitching effect on them both. Marc's air of stiff reserve fell away as he and Leah discovered how much they had in common—a love of horses, old movies, photography and basketball.

"I've never met a woman who could quote NBA statistics like a bookie before," Marc said delightedly, toying with the spoon in his coffee.

"I've mentioned my cousin Mary. Her brothers and mine made sure I learned the finer points of the game. They were always a player or two short of a team. If I didn't fill in, they'd threaten to roll me up and use me as their ball. All their chatter obviously sank in."

"It must have been nice to have a large family while you were growing up. Cousins, aunts and uncles..." Marc looked pensive. "My father was an only child. My mother had one older sister who never married. Our family reunions were nothing to brag about."

Leah tried to imagine Marc as a boy. The image was that of a beautiful, serious child who'd grown up too soon. A life full of grown-ups, responsibility and burden. She couldn't envy his wealth; he'd paid too dear a price for it.

He reached for his water glass and their hands touched. Leah felt a quiver of electricity pass between them. But it wasn't until they were leaving the restaurant that Leah realized some sort of transformation had occurred during dinner. What kind of magic had Ariana worked on her brother? On both of them? They were beginning to act like a couple.

"Should we take a drive?" Marc inclined his head toward the car. "It's only nine o'clock. I don't want to arrive at the house until after Ariana's gone to bed. I'm not up to the third degree tonight."

"And you'll sneak off tomorrow before she wakes up, leaving *me* to answer her questions," Leah accused, wagging a finger at him. Marc caught the finger and, with excessive care, lifted her hand to his mouth to lay a gentle kiss upon her palm.

Leah's throat constricted. She might have pulled her hand away if a delicious languor hadn't overtaken her. "Speaking of Ariana," she choked out, "I wanted to talk to you about her schedule."

Marc gave her a look filled with amusement. "Are you trying to change the subject?" he asked, opening the passenger door for her.

Flustered, Leah shook her head as she got into the car. "I'd like to see Ariana leave the house occasionally. She needs to know there is another world out there...."

"Why?" Chin jutting forward stubbornly, he slid into his own seat. "The only thing there for her is pain."

"For the reasons you gave me tonight! You and Ariana have no one except each other. What if something happened to you, Marc? What if you couldn't take care of her anymore. Do you realize how terrified she'd be, if the first time she ever ventured out of the cocoon you've created for her, she had to do it without you?"

"She would be looked after. There's plenty of money for that."

"That's not my point. She needs to be introduced to the world so that she's not afraid of it. Many Down Syndrome children grow up to hold jobs, Marc."

"What kind of job could Ariana hold?" His tone was brittle.

"Something in a sheltered workshop or a factory that hires the handicapped. There are lots of options."

"None of which are suitable for my sister."

"Think about it, Marc. Please?"

When he looked at her, Leah was taken aback by the anguish on his face. "I promised my parents I would take care of her just as they would have done, Leah. I promised. I'm a man of my word. I pride myself on that. My mother devoted her life to Ariana's welfare. I'm not about to throw that plan in the trash now."

"Even if the plan isn't the best one for your sister?"

His face hardened. "Don't push, Leah. I can't do it. I just can't."

THE WEEK HAD BEEN fairly routine and quiet until, on Friday night, the front door slammed with such force that the watercolors on Leah's bedroom walls shook. Marc's usually controlled voice roared up the stairs and through her door.

"Mrs. Bright! My dress shirts! Has the laundry delivered them yet?"

Leah stole from her room to peer curiously down into the foyer.

Marc and Mrs. Bright stood in the center of the peacock mosaic, haloed by the soft evening light. Mrs. Bright nervously curled her hands together as Marc tugged at his silk tie with his left hand while his right worked the buttons of his shirt. Two buttons popped off and rolled across the tiles. "Damn!" When he turned to look up at Leah, she could see bronzed skin beneath his shirt.

"Something wrong?" Leah murmured with exquisite understatement as she descended the stairs.

Marc glared at her, the closest target for his frustration. "My secretary's head is on the block for this one." He pulled the tails of his shirt from his pants to dangle over his hips. Then he turned his full attention to the still-knotted tie. "I asked her to set up an evening for dinner and drinks with a potential client the firm has been wooing. She neglected to tell me—until forty minutes ago—that the dinner engagement was tonight."

He glared at his watch. "I'm supposed to meet Harrington in an hour, and I don't even have a clean shirt!"

"Can't you wear the one you've got on?" Leah asked.

"With a tux? Hardly. Harrington is a patron of the arts. We'll meet them for a quick dinner, then we're going to the theater. There's a party afterward." He grimaced. "I hate these phony get-togethers—not what I had in mind. They're usually jousting matches to see who can outimpress everyone else with pretentious opinions. I'd rather sit at a stoplight."

"I'll call the laundry," Mrs. Bright assured him. "I'm sure the deliveryman is on his way."

Marc assessed Leah from head to toe, a hungry look in his eyes. "Harrington said I should bring a date."

A shiver of anticipation shot through her.

"I know this is an absolutely lousy thing to do to you, Leah, but I'm in a pinch. Harrington is probably the single most important client my firm has ever sought. I'd like to humor him." His expression grew warm. "Besides, I enjoyed our visit to the sculpture garden—and the restaurant. Would you give me a repeat performance?''

It was undeniably flattering to have Marc court her like this. And she loved the theater. He seemed utterly genuine in his reference to the previous Saturday. Did he really want her to go with him? Or was he just applying some of that devastating charm because he needed a date and she was handy?

"Marc, I...I have twigs in my hair!" She tugged a blond curl. "We've just come in from the garden. Look at me—I'm a mess! I couldn't be ready in time. Besides, I have nothing to wear..."

The intent expression on his face convinced her that it might be prudent to accept his invitation, twigs and all.

"I do love the theater," she admitted wistfully. "And I haven't had much opportunity to go. I've got a black dress that might be all right...."

"You have fifteen minutes to get ready. I'll meet you down here." Marc grabbed her hands in his own and she felt his strong warmth permeate her chilled fingers. "Thank you, Leah. Really." His lips brushed feather-light over her forehead. "Fifteen minutes. No more."

She watched him ascend the staircase and disappear into his room. Feeling as though she'd been picked up and deposited in Oz by an errant tornado, Leah followed.

Her trip through the shower lasted all of two minutes. Her makeup took another five and her hair, seven more. That left one to pull her dress over her head, pluck her shoes out of the closet and walk downstairs. Leah was still trying to finish closing her zipper when Marc brushed away her hands and neatly closed the last few inches. When he put his hands on her shoulders and spun her around, she felt a rush of dizziness.

"You look lovely." His eyes traveled over her simple black sheath with warm approval. He raised a finger to play with the teardrop diamond in her earlobe. "Perfect."

"My hair will have to finish drying in the car. I hope your friend Harrington likes the tousled look," Leah babbled, unnerved by his touch.

Marc had worked some miracles of his own. He was freshly shaved and showered, looking bandbox crisp in a black tux and shoes polished more brightly than mirrors. His dark hair and eyes were enhanced by the whiteness of his shirt. Leah had never seen him more appealing. When he offered her his arm, she hesitantly curled her hand into the crook of his elbow. She and Ariana had been digging in the garden and there hadn't been time for even a touch-up manicure. Her work-roughened fingers were a reminder that his Cinderella story couldn't have a happy ending. She was an imposter.

Imposter!

The thought ricocheted through Leah's mind as they drove toward their destination. The very words had an accusing ring. Who was she fooling, playing dress-up and attending a dinner with Marc? This client, Harrington, might be deceived for the moment, but the one who mattered most knew this "date" was only an act.

"Why so quiet?" Marc asked. "You look as if you'd lost your best friend. Relax." An attractive smile lifted the corners of his mouth. "Frankly I've become rather jaded and bored with these social functions, but I think I'm going to enjoy this evening more than I'd anticipated. Thank you, Leah, for joining me."

Leah settled into the leather cushions of the Porsche and expelled a short, gusty breath. Perhaps this evening would contain a little magic, after all.

CHAPTER FOUR

OTTO HARRINGTON was an imposing man, three hundred pounds of wit, intimidation and insight. Fortunately for Leah, Mr. Harrington, who was farm-born and -reared, proclaimed her the most fascinating person he'd met in years.

"I can't tell you how refreshing it is to meet someone who can relate to life on a farm, Leah," he said expansively, leaning back in his chair as their dishes were cleared away. "Sometimes, when I'm sitting in traffic, watching the news on my car television and my car phone rings, I think I only imagined growing up in a place where roosters woke me up in the morning and the sound of chirruping crickets put me to sleep at night." Harrington skewered Marc with his gaze. "Hang on to this one, Adams. You may never find another quite like her."

Marc smiled easily, obviously comfortable in such situations, and placed his hand possessively over hers. "I'm sure of that, Mr. Harrington. Leah's the only one of her kind."

A meddlesome nanny, you mean, Leah thought, and turned to glare at Marc, but both men's attention was on Mrs. Harrington as she returned from the restaurant lobby.

"I just finished talking to Lucy and she says the play's simply wonderful. Everyone is going to be at the party!" Leah knew "Lucy" was Lucy Walfred, the Virginia playwright whose work they were seeing tonight.

"Since we have a car," Marc suggested, "why don't Leah and I meet you at the theater?"

"Lovebirds want to be alone for a few minutes, eh?" Harrington said jovially. "Can't say I blame you." He wagged his bushy eyebrows at his wife. "Can you, lovey?"

"Let the young people be, dear," Mrs. Harrington scolded lightly. "We should leave for the theater soon. The play starts in less than half an hour."

Marc took the cue. "At the theater, then."

As swiftly as he moved, he still couldn't avoid Mr. Harrington's last-minute advice. "Don't stop somewhere with that young beauty and forget where you're supposed to be tonight, Adams. I have a number of people I'd like you to meet."

"I apologize for what he was insinuating, Leah," Marc said grimly when they were alone. "I hadn't planned a quick stop at a cheap motel, although that's what he seemed to be suggesting. I ought to—"

"You introduced me as your date, after all. Perhaps you should have told him I was the nanny."

"That would have been a little difficult to explain, don't you think?" Some of Marc's good humor returned. "Then I would've had to explain why I have a nanny but no wife or children . . . You're right. This way is easier. Besides—" he grinned beguilingly at her "—Harrington thinks you're the best thing since sliced bread. Who knows? Maybe we'll get this account on the strength of his affection for you." A new look came into his eyes. "Then you'd have to stay on as Ariana's nanny for the sake of my business."

First Harrington, now Marc himself, talking of a connection, a commitment between Marc and her. Leah didn't want to think about it. She liked to deal only in dreams that had some chance of becoming reality.

THE PLAY, though slightly esoteric for her tastes, was a success. Three curtain calls and a standing ovation later, Marc and Leah walked slowly through backstage corridors to the site of the party. The Harringtons had hurried ahead to congratulate their friend Lucy, leaving Marc and Leah to find their own way.

As they traversed a long hallway, Marc put his hand on her arm and pulled her aside, his expression thoughtful. "Perhaps I should warn you, Leah, that there may be people at this party I've known in the past."

She gave him a puzzled glance.

"That's to be expected. Your family's been on the Washington scene for a long time."

"What I mean is, my ex-wife often comes to these things."

That bit of news left Leah speechless.

"She can be something of a shrew," he said with a resigned shake of his head. "Of course, she can also be very charming. I felt I should let you know—just in case."

Leah experienced a sinking sensation in the pit of her stomach. Marc's ex-wife! She wasn't prepared to meet the woman face-to-face or, worse, be compared to her in any way. The very thought tarnished her lovely evening.

Marc, however, was calm about the situation. "We generally handle ourselves civilly at this kind of event. No use airing dirty laundry for the Washington gossips. She's learned to retract her claws in public." He chuckled dryly. "Mind you, she still has them—and I know how sharp they can be."

"Here goes," he muttered as he steered her toward bright lights and bouquets of glittering balloons at the far end of the hall.

They catapulted from the darkness into an ocean of light, people and laughter. The chatter died away for a moment as the party goers studied the latest addition to their group. Leah's apprehension grew. Mr. Harrington bore down on them clutching a glass of champagne.

"There you are! Took your time getting here, didn't you?" He winked at them. "Don't blame you. Things are just warming up now. Come on. There are people I want you to meet."

Marc moved easily through the crowd, working it as deftly as an experienced politician. There were many familiar faces which Leah recognized from television and the newspaper. She tried to suppress her nervousness by playing a silent game of "name that face."

Ever the perfect escort, Marc introduced her to everyone, slipping comfortably into the polished chitchat of cocktail parties.

"Adams! I've been meaning to talk to you." A dignified older gentleman hurried toward them. "I wanted your opinion on the Hanson-Bonner ruling that came down last week. Do you think it will have a big impact?"

Marc murmured something in unintelligible legalese that seemed to please the other man. He slapped Marc on the shoulder and asked, "May I quote you on that?" Leah was awed by the respect Marc appeared to command in this diverse social group. Obviously Otto Harrington was impressed, too.

She noticed how comfortable Marc was among important people like these and how well he fit in. It was a potent reminder that, despite his comments to the contrary, he'd given up a great deal when he became Ariana's guardian.

"Well, how did we do?" Leah asked him as they surveyed the food-laden table. "Do we get the job?"

"Who knows?" Marc appeared unconcerned. "Shrimp?" He speared a tiny pink curl with a decorated toothpick and teased Leah's lower lip with it.

"Adams! Ms. Brock, I have someone here I'd like you to meet!" Unknowingly Mr. Harrington shattered the moment. "This is Lucy Walfred, star of the evening. Lucy, I'd like you to meet Marc Adams, my new attorney."

Neither Marc nor Leah missed the significance of Harrington's introduction. After he and Lucy Walfred drifted away, Leah discreetly raised two fingers in a victory sign.

"I guess I can enjoy the party now," Marc said as he heaped a pile of shrimp onto his plate. "Let's find a corner where I can feed you this. I rather liked it." He was staring avidly at Leah's mouth.

Shrimp and champagne in hand, they'd just settled behind a floating cluster of congratulatory balloons when a flurry of excitement exploded through the room. Leah glanced up to see who had arrived.

She would have known the man anywhere. Blake Evans was the country's current heartthrob. That handsome face hawked sports cars and athletic equipment on prime-time commercials and broke hearts on a popular soap opera every afternoon. She was so engrossed in staring at Blake Evans and the beautiful dark-haired woman on his arm that Leah was surprised to hear Marc mutter an expletive.

"Marc!" She turned to speak to him, but the words never came. His lips were pressed tightly together. He tossed back the rest of his champagne and signaled to a nearby waiter for more.

"Do you know him?" Leah asked hesitantly.

"Maybe we should leave, Leah. We've accomplished what we came here to do. If I can just get rid of this plate..." Before he could move, a smooth, husky voice assailed them.

"Well, isn't this a surprise? I didn't know you did parties anymore, Marc."

Leah looked up to see the stunning woman who'd entered on Blake Evans's arm. She was a classic beauty— flawless ivory skin, raven hair swept back from a delicate widow's peak, icy blue eyes that could probably freeze water, and full sensuous lips. Her low-cut strapless dress was a miracle of design engineering.

"Hello, Trina." Marc's voice was low and contained, as though he were addressing a stranger.

"It's been simply ages, Marc. You're looking well." Trina slithered closer. She leaned forward to give him an even more panoramic view of her chest.

"Thanks. So are you."

All of you, Leah thought grumpily. Who was this woman, anyway? What was she to Marc?

"Introduce me to your friend." Trina turned toward Leah with a surprisingly sincere smile. "Socializing is quite a change for you."

Marc ignored the curious gibe. "Leah Brock, I'd like you to meet Trina—" he hesitated a moment "—Michaels. Trina, this is Leah Brock."

Trina gave a tinkling laugh. "Have you forgotten, Marc? I kept the name." Trina extended a hand, her red-lacquered nails glittering in the light. "I'm Trina *Adams.* Marc's wife."

Leah felt incredibly stupid. Of course this was Marc's wife! And obviously he didn't want the two of them to meet.

"*Ex*-wife, Trina." Marc's dark eyes sparked with irritation. "Or have *you* forgotten?"

"I could never forget you, Marc. There are certain things a woman will always remember. Her first love is always at the top of the list. Don't you think so, Leah?"

There was a naughty impishness about the question that caught Leah off guard. She nearly smiled.

Marc grabbed Leah's elbow, forcing her to her feet. "We'd love to stay and chat, Trina, but Leah and I were just on our way home. Now if you'd excuse us . . ."

"So soon? You haven't changed completely. Still a homebody. How is—"

"Fine, thanks. Although I'm surprised you asked."

"Give me *some* credit, Marc!" Leah could sense that Trina was genuinely upset about Marc's abrupt statement. "You're so unreasonable where she's concerned!"

"That's the pot calling the kettle black!"

Leah stared from Marc to Trina and back again. What on earth were they talking—no, fighting about? It couldn't be Ariana, could it?

Leah's feet barely touched the ground as Marc propelled her through the room to say their thank-yous to the Harringtons. It wasn't until they reached the car that Marc eased the death grip he had on her arm. He helped Leah into her seat, then stalked around the car and slid inside.

He sat there, unmoving, for a long moment. The blue-gray fluorescent lighting of the garage cast ragged angry shadows across his features. Finally he started the car, stomped on the accelerator and drove into the street.

After several minutes, Leah realized they weren't heading directly toward his house. It wasn't until he pulled into the parking lot of an old-fashioned all-night diner that she dared to ask, "Where are we?"

"Big Dave's. I used to come here as a kid. Best beef stew west of the Atlantic." He grinned faintly. "Okay, it's not the greatest beef stew, but I like it. Come on."

Leah felt overdressed for the tile-and-plastic interior of the diner, but there were only three customers, high-school boys playing an ancient pinball machine.

"I didn't know places like this still existed!" she gasped, feeling as though she'd stepped out of the Porsche and into the past.

A burly man in a grease-spotted apron slammed two water glasses on the table in front of them as they settled into a booth. "What'll you have—the usual? Two beef stews? Extra rolls?" He eyed Marc. "And a large milk. Good for ulcers. Didn't I always tell you that lawyering would give you ulcers?" Without waiting for a reply the man stalked away.

"Dave?" Leah asked.

"In the flesh. I've been coming here all my life."

Dave reappeared with two huge bowls of beef stew, a heaping mound of fresh rolls and two quart-size glasses of milk. "You'll have pie for dessert," he decreed. "Apple." With that, he turned and left.

"What if you didn't want apple?" Leah whispered.

"You'd eat it, anyway. Dave hates to see food go to waste."

Though she hadn't thought she was hungry, Leah found herself devouring the savory stew and mopping up the remains with a fluffy roll. When they were finished eating, she leaned back and watched Marc. "Comfort food," she said, pressing her hands on her stomach.

"Hmm?" He was spooning apple pie into his mouth.

"Comfort food. The kind of food you eat when things go wrong. Food that makes you think of your childhood and Mom in the kitchen, baking. My comfort foods are roast beef with mashed potatoes, homemade rolls and vanilla pudding decorated with bananas and vanilla wafers. Comfort food."

He chuckled. "You're absolutely right. Good old Dave has pulled me through more than one crisis over the years."

"Want to talk about it?" she ventured, feeling very bold.

"About Trina, you mean?" He shrugged. "There's nothing to say. We were married. It didn't work. We were divorced. End of subject."

Leah wished it was that simple. There had been some kind of negative energy between Marc and Trina—hot and potent and dangerous.

"You look like a balloon that's just been poked with a pin," Leah commented. "Deflated."

Marc picked up the bubble-glass saltshaker and rolled it between his palms.

"What happened—" Leah stopped herself before she would regret the words. "Never mind. It's none of my business."

He regarded her speculatively for a long moment. "To our marriage, you mean?" He weighed his words carefully, as if finally recalling his employer-employee relationship with Leah. "I suppose you should know."

"I didn't mean to pry. It's really none of my business...."

"It might be. It has to do with Ariana." He carefully set the saltshaker down and started drumming his fingers on the tabletop.

"Trina and I met during my final semester in Boston." A rueful grin slanted one side of his mouth. "There was a lot of...electricity between us." He held her gaze. "Frankly, we were good in bed together and stayed there most of my final term."

Leah's mouth went dry and she hurriedly reached for another sip of milk.

"We decided that any chemistry that good should be cultivated. Trina and I married the day before my parents arrived for graduation." A hooded look darkened his eyes. "My mistake. Haste makes waste."

"Didn't your parents like her?" Leah wondered.

"They liked her just fine. I was besotted with her. What could they do? The trouble didn't start until Trina met Ariana."

"Ariana? How could she cause trouble?"

"Trina has no tolerance for imperfect people."

An image of Trina Adams's extraordinary beauty, flawless voice and intimidating poise flickered through Leah's mind. On the surface, at least, Trina Adams *was* perfect. Suddenly Marc's statement made painful sense.

"Ariana frightened her?"

"Frightened. Repulsed. Disgusted. Whatever. Trina wanted nothing to do with a handicapped child." Marc scraped his fingers through his hair. "What made it even worse was the fact that Ariana adored Trina. She couldn't stop staring at her, trying to touch her. She thought Trina was the most beautiful thing she'd ever seen."

Leah could just imagine it. Ariana clinging to the one person who wanted nothing to do with her.

"I didn't even think to warn Trina about Ariana. I brought her to the house and introduced her to my sister without mentioning that Ariana was retarded. I look back now and wonder at my stupidity, but at the time, all I thought about was Trina and..."

Leah was able to fill in the blank.

"Trina has an almost pathological fear of imperfection," he went on. "If I had a cold or a sore throat, she'd insist on not seeing me until I was better. Discussions about diseases sent her up the wall. To have Ariana sprung on her, well, it was too much."

Too much! Leah was dumbfounded. Now she could see how the marriage might have fallen apart. She experienced a wave of sympathy for both of them. Still, she couldn't help saying, "But Ariana is a lovely child, Marc."

"Not everyone has your attitude, Leah. There's a prejudice out there that I'd never considered. Trina tried, but it wasn't enough. When my parents were killed and I knew I'd have to take care of Ariana myself..."

"The marriage was over?"

"She didn't even move into the house with me. An old friend from law school handled the divorce."

Leah's heart hurt when she looked at him. He'd given up so much for his family, for his sister—his career in New York, his social life, his freedom, his wife. How could he even begin to tally what he'd lost?

CHAPTER FIVE

SATURDAY PASSED QUIETLY, with Marc at the office working on a legal brief. On Sunday Leah made a trip to her apartment to gather more clothing, answer her mail and have tea with her roommate. Leah had been feeling guilty about leaving Christina alone in their apartment, but Christina, an artist, had covered every free inch of wall with her canvases and seemed pleased enough to have the extra space. By the time she returned to the Adams household, Leah was happier, even though she hadn't yet sorted out her feelings about Marc or the former Mrs. Adams.

"They're in the garden." Mrs. Bright pointed toward the backyard when Leah entered the kitchen.

Leah walked through the French doors in time to hear Marc say, "You've planted every seedling left in the greenhouse. Don't you think it's time to rest?" Marc, dressed in moss-green chinos and a white polo shirt, dusted off his hands and surveyed their day's work.

Ariana, who'd attracted a great deal more dirt than her brother, brushed worriedly at her blue jeans. "They're dirty, Marc. Can we wash them?"

"I'll throw them in the machine while you bathe," Leah offered, announcing her presence.

"You're back!" Ariana clapped her hands. "Can you wash them now?"

Marc gave his sister a little push. "Have Mrs. Bright help you with the tub. When Leah gets over that warm welcome, she'll take care of your jeans."

He looked particularly attractive today, Leah observed. Casual clothes did wonders for his physique, and Leah found herself wishing he'd wear them more often.

"Lemonade?" Marc indicated the patio table, which held a frosted pitcher and three glasses. He'd just finished filling Leah's glass when Mrs. Bright bustled out of the kitchen carrying a plate of dainty sandwiches and a bowl of sliced fruit.

"You wore the poor child out. Ariana's nearly asleep in the bathtub. So I'll let her eat in her room. I thought you and Leah might like a light supper here on the porch."

"How was your day off?" Marc asked politely as they seated themselves at the table. He made no reference to the "date" two nights before.

"Great. I accomplished everything I needed to do and even had time to visit a friend. I'm ready for another week."

"A friend?" His brow furrowed and a shadow of understanding crept across his features. "I'm sorry, Leah. I must be very single-minded. It never occurred to me that you'd like time away from here to see your—" he paused before putting an odd inflection in the last word "—friends. Would you like some evenings off? Just say so if you do."

He meant men friends! "There's no need. There's no one I can't visit on a Sunday." She smiled ruefully. "I was referring to my roommate."

Marc's dark eyes flickered. "I thought there might be someone special in your life, someone you wanted to see more than once a week." His expression and tone were openly curious. For an instant Leah wished there was a man she could mention—to let Marc know that her love life was not a complete void.

"Not at the moment," she murmured.

"There has been, then? In the past, I mean."

"Off and on. Nothing serious."

Marc flushed deeply. "I'm sorry. I had no right to ask. After the other night when I spilled out my guts to you . . ."

"It's all right. I've been very focused—first on school, then on establishing my agency. There never seems to be time for more." A delicate smile curved her lips. "My family accuses me of having tunnel vision where my life is concerned."

"I suppose we're all guilty of that occasionally." Suddenly, as if wary of where the conversation might lead, Marc slapped his hands. "I'm still hungry. How about you? Let's see what Mrs. Bright has in the kitchen."

They crept furtively into the darkened room. "Should we be doing this?" Leah whispered, feeling like a naughty schoolgirl. "Everything's so perfect here. We'd better not make a mess."

"It's my house. I should be able to—" he stopped short, staring into a cupboard. "Do you realize this woman alphabetizes the spices?"

"And irons the dish towels?"

"And labels leftovers in calligraphy?"

Marc opened the refrigerator door, his muscular shape outlined by its light. "I've got that woman working in the wrong place! She should be in my office. She could teach the secretaries a thing or two."

"Who'd take care of us?" Leah protested.

The banter continued as they scoured the kitchen for sweets. When they were done, their loot included a can of fudge sauce, a package of peanuts, a jar of cherries and canister of powdered malt.

"What can we do with this?" Marc puzzled. "Chocolate soup?" He wiped his hands on his pants. "Maybe I should clean up first."

Leah gently shoved him toward the door. "Go take a shower. I'll work it out." While he was gone, Leah dished up ice cream, sprinkled it with a dash of malt, then sprinkled peanuts and drizzled fudge sauce over the top. As she worked, she thought about Marc and his sister.

In spite of the wonderful home Marc had provided, Ariana needed independence. Not in large doses, of course, but enough to give her inner resources to rely on. Because if anything were to happen to Marc . . .

Ariana needed friends, responsibilities. Leah's cousin Mary had blossomed when she was hired to work at a sheltered workshop. Leah could imagine Ariana experiencing the same wonderful pride of accomplishment. What she couldn't imagine was Marc approving of changes like this.

He returned just as Leah placed a cherry on top of his sundae.

"Looks good!" he said, smiling and rumpling his still-damp hair with his fingers. He'd changed into white cotton trousers and a navy-and-white-striped shirt. He was sockless in his deck shoes. Leah felt an unwelcome ripple of attraction. It was apparent in his eyes that he'd felt it, too. The electricity between them made her senses reel as he put his hands on her shoulders and dragged them slowly down her arms. "Leah, I—"

The sound of chimes interrupted him.

Never before had Leah been so disappointed to hear a doorbell ring. Never before had she seen a man move so quickly to answer one.

Leah placed the sundaes on a tray and carried them to the study. When she reached the foyer, she found Marc there—but not alone.

"Leah," he called to her, "I'd like you to meet Melanie Dean. Ms. Dean has worked in my office for the past six months. Melanie, Leah looks after my sister. She's her nanny."

Melanie Dean was a pretty young woman under her overstated makeup. The slash of deep-red lipstick and layers of thick black mascara were a stark contrast to her milky white complexion and sleek black hair. She bore a stunning resemblance to Trina Adams.

Melanie surveyed Leah with disdainful eyes. Leah was suddenly and acutely aware of her ancient sweatshirt and faded madras shorts.

Melanie briefly inclined her head toward Leah and then dismissed her. Clearly a nanny was not worthy of her attention.

"Marc," Melanie continued, as if Leah hadn't entered, "I've been working on this Hockstettler case all weekend and I've just discovered some case law that will tip this thing in our favor. I want your go-ahead before I pursue it any further. I found this in Farmington versus . . ."

Leah stood awkwardly in the hallway as Marc and Melanie moved into the formal living room, their heads bent together over the folders in Melanie's hand. Leah's self-esteem began to melt right along with the ice cream sundaes.

She recognized Melanie Dean as a predatory sort of woman. Not only that, Ms. Dean was seriously infatuated with Marc; Leah sensed it immediately. She also realized that as soon as Ms. Dean had heard the word "nanny," she hadn't even bothered to go in for the kill. Nannies weren't competition. They were like pieces of furniture or kitchen appliances, necessary to run a household but of no further account.

Whatever had made her think she might be important here? Leah wondered glumly. She was an employee, nothing more—no matter how many times Marc took her to dinner, revealed truths about his past or shared laughter with her over a kitchen counter. Just as Leah decided to ask Mrs. Bright if she were interested in a slightly soupy sundae, Marc called her.

"Leah! Bring that ice cream in here!"

"We were about to eat these, Melanie. Would you care for one?" Marc asked politely as Leah padded barefoot into the room. He plucked a bowl off the tray.

"Ice cream?" Melanie shook her head emphatically and smoothed a hand across her concave middle. "Too many calories."

"More for us then, I guess. Sit down, Leah," Marc instructed. "Melanie and I will be done in a minute."

Leah felt Melanie's eyes inspecting her, from tousled hair to tanned bare feet.

"I'm, uh, sorry if I interrupted anything," Melanie said cattily, her attention locked on Leah's big toe.

Marc followed her gaze. "It's Leah's day off."

"And she spends it here? With you?" Disapproval oozed from every syllable.

Marc seemed not to have heard the question. He gathered the papers and handed them to Melanie. "Keep working with this. I think you're on to something. I'll take a look at it tomorrow morning. Are you sure you don't want some ice cream?"

Melanie backed toward the door, shooting Leah a hostile glare.

When Marc returned from seeing her out, a faint smile tugged at the corners of his lips. "Ms. Dean is a good worker. Seven days a week, fifteen hours a day. She's the only person in the office who doesn't leave at night until I do." Marc dropped onto the couch across from Leah and picked up his sundae. "Something wrong?"

Surely he could see that Melanie was possessive and territorial where he was concerned. The woman was in love with him!

"No. Just thinking." *Thinking I don't blame that woman for falling in love with you. Thinking I'd do it in a minute if our situation was different.* Listlessly Leah ate her sundae and returned the dish to the tray.

"It seems awfully quiet here tonight," Marc observed companionably. "Care for a game of cards?"

"Thanks, but no thanks. I'm very tired," she lied. "I should probably go to bed."

Was there a flicker of disappointment in those dark eyes?

"Whatever you say. Good night then, Leah."

"Good night . . . Marc."

As she mounted the stairs to her room, Leah mourned the friendly relationship she'd let slip away. If only things were different. But they weren't. She was a nanny. Marc Adams was her employer. Period.

LEAH RUMMAGED through the drawers of her bathroom vanity as Ariana perched on the edge of the stool, highly interested in the proceedings. "No toothpaste. Do you have any, Ariana?"

"Nope. I used it all. See?" She flashed a wide, toothy smile at Leah.

"Lovely. But I really can't function without toothpaste. I suppose I'll have to walk to that little pharmacy and pick some up."

"Me, too?" Ariana's eyes brightened hopefully.

It had been a long day for both of them. Marc had left before breakfast without so much as a goodbye. Because Mrs. Bright had complained of a headache, they'd tried to stay out of her way as much as possible. That left Leah and Ariana tiptoeing around the house, bored and restless.

"I don't know, honey. Your brother says—"

"Marc's not home."

"True, but he's the one who makes the rules in this house."

"Too many rules."

Leah relented. "Oh, why not? It's only four or five blocks. You can walk that far."

"What's a block?"

This poor seventeen-year-old city dweller didn't even know what a block was! Leah made up her mind. "Put on your tennis shoes. We can be there and back in less than half an hour."

"YOU'RE DOING WHAT?" Mrs. Bright clutched a cold compress to her head and gave a sickly groan. "You can't. Mr. Marc won't stand for it."

"Marc's not home," Ariana repeated. "We don't have toothpaste."

"Leave her here with me, Leah. Take the car. Please."

"It's a lovely day. A walk will be good for both of us. Besides, you need to rest."

"I won't rest if you take that child out of the house," Mrs. Bright wailed. "Mr. Marc—"

"I'll worry about Marc. You just put your feet up for a bit. We'll be back shortly." Leah prevailed. Mrs. Bright reluctantly leaned against the pillows on the family-room couch.

"Just remember, I said I disapproved."

"I won't forget." Leah took Ariana by the elbow. "Come on, honey. Let's go."

The four-block trip to the pharmacy might have been an around-the-world cruise as far as Ariana was concerned. "What's that?" she pointed right, then left. "And that?"

"A police car, a boy on a skateboard and an American flag. Haven't you seen those things before?" Leah asked gently.

"On TV. Oh! A penny!" Ariana dove for a copper penny glinting on the sidewalk. She clutched it as though it were pirate's booty. "I've got a penny!"

Ariana wanted to stop and touch every leaf, smell every flower and stare at every stop sign. And the pharmacy was even more distracting. Leah finally settled Ariana before a display of glass and prisms while she purchased her toothpaste. Ariana was still rooted to the spot when she returned.

"Can I have one, Leah?" Ariana gazed longingly at the bits of glass sparkling in the light. "That one!" She indicated a tear drop-shaped crystal. It was tiny but multifaceted and strung on a piece of plastic thread.

Leah looked at the awed expression on the girl's face and her heart melted.

All the way to the house, Ariana clutched the crystal in her hand, transfixed by the treasure she held.

Leah felt a lump form in her throat. How little it took to please this child! How easy it would be to devote her life to doing just that....

Leah and Ariana held hands as they walked up the curving driveway to the house. Ariana hummed tunelessly and Leah felt a bit like singing herself. The little outing had created an almost magical bond between them. But their mood shattered when they stepped into the house.

"Where have you been?" Marc descended from the second floor in a raging fury.

"Look, Marc!" Ariana vainly opened her hand to show him her treasure.

"How dare you take her off the grounds!" He stalked toward Leah with such ferocity that she took a step backward.

"We just went to pick up some toothpaste—"

Marc cut her off. "She doesn't belong outside the gardens!"

"There was no traffic. We only saw a few people...."

"Marc, I know what prisms are now—"

"You've gone to far, Leah. You can't be trusted."

Again, Ariana tried to placate her brother. "Don't be mad, Marc. They sparkle in the light."

"Don't be unreasonable," Leah added. "The walk didn't do any damage."

"You had no right!"

"Marc!" Ariana latched onto Marc's sleeve and tugged. "Don't be mad at Leah." Her chin trembled as he turned to her. "I'm scared, Marc."

"Of course you're scared. Leah shouldn't have taken you out—"

"I'm scared of *you!* Don't yell. It hurts my ears." Ariana clamped her palms to the sides of her head and tears ran from her eyes. "Don't yell at Leah."

Gently Marc laid a hand on his sister's arm. "Ariana, this is something you don't understand. This doesn't have anything to do with you. Leah did something wrong. She disobeyed my orders. Now we'll have to discuss it. Maybe you should go to your room. I don't want you upset."

"She was fine until you started ranting and raving like a madman!" Leah accused angrily. She hurried to Ariana's side and smoothed the girl's silken hair. "Honey, you go upstairs and hang your pretty prism in your window. See how the light shines through it? Marc and I will have a little talk, and then we'll come up to see it."

Ariana looked frantically from Marc to Leah and back again as she moved toward the stairs, tightly gripping her prism.

"Great, just great! You handled that beautifully!" Leah hissed when Ariana disappeared into her bedroom. "You've upset her!"

"*I've* upset her? Who took her shopping?"

"She loved it! We were as happy as anything. Then you had to act like some vengeful god! Ariana wasn't crying when she came into the house. She is now. Who do you suppose caused that?" Marc sagged against the study door and raked his fingers through his hair, and Leah took advantage of his weak moment. "You've done her more harm than good by being so overprotective."

"You know the rules."

"The rules are stupid." Leah's body shook with righteous indignation. "So fire me." The fury in her eyes kept him where he was. "She had a wonderful time, Marc. She saw things she'd never seen before. I had some extra quarters, and we used them to take the tests those little machines offer...."

"She took a stress test?"

Leah covered her mouth to hide a threatening smile. "Actually, she did the 'How Hot a Lover Are You?' one. She put the tips of her fingers on these pads and it tabulated—"

"What am I going to do with you, Leah?" Marc's anger gave way to befuddled astonishment.

"And her blood pressure is normal. After that, I ran out of quarters."

"I give up! I surrender! I can't deal with you!" He glared at her, but a quirk of amusement kept pulling at the corner of his lip. "Just don't take her out like that again. And for heaven's sake, don't give her any more sex quizzes!"

"Maybe I shouldn't have let her, but she thought it was fun." *Fun.* There was that word again, causing her all kinds of trouble.

"I know you don't agree with me, Leah, but I do feel I know what's best for my sister."

Leah faced him boldly. "I apologize for taking her out without prior approval, but I want you to know that next time—and there will be a next time—I'll ask you first. Ariana needs to leave this house!"

At that moment, Mrs. Bright came bustling down the stairs. "Where's Ariana?"

"In her room," Marc and Leah said simultaneously.

"Oh, no she's not." Mrs. Bright shook her head emphatically. "I've been up there cleaning out her drawers. It's quiet as a morgue."

It was an unfortunate choice of words. Marc stared at Leah in dismay. "If she's not upstairs, where is she?"

"We both saw her go up...."

"I didn't hear a thing..." Mrs. Bright supplied.

"Could she have slipped down the back way?"

"But where would she go?"

Leah felt the panic rising in her throat. The fight with Marc, the yelling... What had Ariana been driven to do?

SHE WASN'T in any of the upstairs rooms. In fact, Ariana was nowhere to be found.

They scoured the grounds, peering under the hedges and behind the big old trees. Marc and Leah ransacked the garage while Mrs. Bright checked the toolsheds and the porches. The longer they searched, the more frightened Leah became. She couldn't look at Marc, fearing she'd break into tears if she saw his pale face and dark terrified eyes.

"Where could she have gone?" he muttered. "We were only talking for a few minutes!"

"We were screaming, Marc." And to Ariana, it must have seemed like forever. "Maybe she left the grounds."

He grew even paler.

"The only place she's ever been is the drugstore. Maybe she went back. She loved one of the displays they had."

Leaving Mrs. Bright to stand guard, Marc and Leah raced toward the pharmacy on foot, hoping desperately to see Ariana dawdling along the way.

The druggist was closing the door as they arrived.

"Have you seen a young girl, age seventeen, long blonde hair, blue eyes . . ." Marc took charge.

"Dozens of 'em."

Leah stepped forward. "I was here earlier today with a young woman with Down Syndrome. She was intrigued by the prism display."

"Oh, her! Sure I remember her. Megawatt smile. Sweet little thing. She told me I had pretty eyes." The aging man grinned. "First time in years anybody under the age of fifty has had something nice to say to me."

"Did she come back?"

"Nope. I would have remembered. Sorry." As they turned away he called after them. "Hope you find her. This city is no place for a young girl alone after dark."

Marc broke into a jog. "We have to get back to the house. It's time to call the police."

"I don't think—"

"You're damn right you don't!" All his fury and fear descended on Leah. "Or none of this would have happened. We need the police."

Leah bit her lip and kept pace with him. He was right. Ariana had to be found immediately. Mounting an all-out search throughout the area would find Ariana, if running away had been her plan. However, knowing Ariana as she did, Leah believed that the girl hadn't meant to go far from home.

She'd obviously wanted to escape the conflict between Marc and Leah, but leave home? It didn't make sense. Ariana loved her home, the gardens, her family. But where could she have gone?

Mrs. Bright was sobbing on the front step when they arrived. Marc brushed past her to the telephone, while Leah stopped to comfort the distraught woman. Within five minutes the wail of police sirens rent the evening air.

The officer who came to the door was brisk and impersonal. "Missing person, sir? We usually wait twenty-four hours, but if she's retarded, that's different. If you'd give us a description..."

Leah sat miserably as Marc described his sister in careful detail. She hadn't realized how closely Marc watched Ariana's day-to-day life. He was able to describe not only her physical appearance, but also the outfit she was wearing, down to the dimes—not pennies—Ariana had insisted Leah insert in the slots of her loafers because she liked their bright silver color.

"Don't worry, sir. If she's out there we'll find her. She can't have gone far. I've radioed for some dogs to help out."

Dogs! Ariana had no experience with animals. Leah could imagine her fright if she thought she was being stalked by snuffling animals and large men in intimidating uniforms.

"Marc, this isn't going to work."

"What choice have we got?" The painful catch in his voice forced Leah to look at him. Her heart twisted when she saw his anguished face.

"This doesn't make sense, Marc. I know Ariana. There's something wrong about all of this."

"You bet there is. In seventeen years, Ariana has never seen or heard anyone argue over her. What's wrong is that I allowed you to provoke me. What's wrong is that you took her out without my permission. And now she's paying the price!"

It would be absolutely no good for both of them to lose their tempers again. Still, Leah needed to make Marc understand that there was a missing piece in this puzzle. She took him by the arm and pulled him off to the side. "Listen to me. I know you're angry and frightened, but the way to find Ariana is by considering *her*."

"You mean you think we aren't?" Marc gestured toward the milling police officers and flashing lights. "I didn't invite these people here for the fun of it." He turned on her like a grizzly bear protecting his territory. "If anyone hasn't considered her needs, it's you!"

Leah ignored his rage, knowing it masked fear. "Let's take this step by step," she said with as much composure as she could muster. "We have to think this through."

"She heard us fighting over her. She ran away. Now she might be in danger. Do you want to think any further than that? I don't." He sat down heavily on the steps and closed his eyes.

"Ariana and I had a wonderful walk to the pharmacy."

"Don't do this, Leah."

"We talked about the sky, the houses, the traffic."

"I can't listen to this now."

"When we returned to the house, she was giddy with excitement. Then, this wonderful adventure was turned into something dreadful by our argument."

"Oh, Lord." Marc dropped his head into his hands.

"She obviously knew she was the cause of the fight."

"I should have kept my mouth shut."

"What would go through Ariana's mind at a time like that? What would she do?" Leah's own mind whirled as she tried to put herself in the girl's place.

"That's obvious. Run away." Marc's tone, though sarcastic, was less hostile.

"But where? The dentist? She'd never go there even if she could remember the way. The pharmacy? We tracked her there. Don't you see, Marc? If Ariana wanted to run away from us, I think she'd run to someplace secure, someplace she knew."

"But we've looked all over the house."

"The house isn't truly her favorite place."

"We've checked the gardens."

"Have we? Really looked, I mean?" Leah's chin took on a determined thrust. "We need to look again." Without thinking, she reached for Marc's hand and pulled him through the house.

In the kitchen they met Mrs. Bright, helplessly wringing her hands as a policeman barked orders into the telephone. "Where are you going?"

"We're checking the back again. Are you sure there was nothing behind the hedges or in the toolsheds?"

"Nothing's been moved. The equipment was covered with those big gray tarps, like always."

"Tarps?" Marc and Leah blurted the word in unison.

"She wouldn't have thought to—"

"Give your sister some credit, Marc!" Leah said sharply as they both rushed off.

The toolsheds, serviceable redwood structures, decorative yet functional, stood at the far corner of the yard. Marc switched on the light in the first shed. Along the far wall, lawn equipment, rakes, hoes and shovels stood at attention like wood and metal soldiers. Buckets and barrels, pots and planters were stacked neatly at the back. There was no place for anything bigger than a mouse to hide.

The other shed, slightly larger, housed two tractor-type lawn mowers carefully shrouded beneath a dingy gray tarp.

"This is crazy, Leah. Mrs. Bright looked in here. You can see for yourself that—"

Ignoring him, Leah slowly pulled the tarp. Huddled between the two mowers, her hair a nest of grass clippings and twigs, was Ariana. She lifted her head to reveal a puffy, tearstained face. Her bottom lip trembled. "Don't be mad, Marc. Leah and I were good."

He was immediately on his knees beside her, touching her face with gentle fingers. "I'm not mad, honey. I never was."

"You and Leah..."

"Were having a very stupid conversation. We didn't mean to frighten you." He stroked her golden hair and rocked back and forth on the balls of his feet.

"We were good, Marc. It was fun. I saw a squirrel and some prisms." Slowly Ariana opened her clenched fist to reveal the tiny piece of crystal Leah had bought her. "See?" A light of pleasure and amazement flickered in her troubled face. "Can I see another one someday?"

If a single look could break a heart, the one Marc gave Leah would have sent hers shattering in a million pieces.

"Sure, honey, you can see another one someday." His words were barely a whisper. He stood, bringing Ariana to her feet with him. Then, as if she were five instead of seventeen, he picked her up and carried her toward the house.

IT WAS VERY LATE by the time the police had finished their last report, Mrs. Bright had cried out the last of her panicked tears, and Ariana had bathed, eaten and fallen asleep. Leah left the kitchen and walked softly toward the study. She stepped through the door into the dimly lit room. The only light was cast by a small lamp on Marc's desk, illuminating little and throwing him into stark shadow.

He looked more weary and vulnerable than she'd seen him. His shirt was open at the collar and his hair was rumpled. It took all of Leah's restraint not to wrap him in her arms and comfort him the way he'd comforted Ariana only a little while before.

"Sit down." He gestured at the chair across from him. "We need to talk."

Leah's stomach turned to lead and dropped toward the soles of her feet. Woodenly she obeyed.

"Are you all right?"

"Are *you?*"

He smiled weakly. "Not yet, but I will be. I think. I hope."

Leah couldn't stay in the chair. Impulsively she rose and moved around the desk to grasp his hand. "I want to apologize. I can't tell you how awful I feel about what happened today. I love Ariana and I'm the last person in the world who wants her to suffer in any way. Please believe that."

When he remained silent, Leah continued, "I never dreamed that such an innocent trip could get so wildly out of hand. I failed both you and Ariana. I'm sorry. I know you'll want me to leave. I don't blame you."

Leah was stunned when, instead of agreeing, Marc growled, "No!" and pulled her closer so quickly that she fell awkwardly into his lap.

"I'm the one who's sorry." His voice was muffled by her shoulder. "You understood her better than I did. I sent up the flames and sounded the alarms. *You* sat back and considered Ariana."

Leah realized with a start that she was running her fingers through his hair. It was short and thick and silky.

"Don't leave us. Ariana couldn't tolerate that."

Leah sagged against his chest, and soon her breathing matched his. His all-male scent surrounded her and she felt a knot of desire burn within her.

"I don't know..."

"You have to know. We need you, Leah. We all need you."

The love she felt for him was an almost physical pain, tightening around her heart. She wanted him in the most basic, elemental way a woman could want a man. She wanted him to be hers.

But what had he said? *We need you. We all need you.* He needed her, all right. So did Ariana. And Mrs. Bright. Did he need her in the same way she needed him? She shifted uneasily on his lap, drawing a startled breath from him.

Marc raised his arms to bury his fingers in her curls. "*I* need you, Leah." He spoke the words against her lips so that she could feel the gentle movement of his lips. "I need you."

Though she succumbed to the rain of kisses he scattered across her mouth, her cheeks, her eyelids, a nagging worry spiraled down into a desperate sinking sensation.

He whispered the words she'd always dreamed of hearing. He needed her. He wanted her. But was it for herself? Or was it because he'd found a woman who truly understood Ariana?

CHAPTER SIX

"YOU WANT TO DO WHAT?" Marc's roar echoed off the walls.

Leah took a step back. She flinched at the sight of his flushed angry face, but didn't retreat from her suggestion. "I think you should enroll Ariana in dance classes." She pulled a photocopied schedule from her pocket. "I picked this up at the Center for the Handicapped. The center is run by a private foundation, Marc. It doesn't have a huge budget, but they have wonderful programs. Clients come there on a pay-what-you-can basis. Because you can afford it, you'd be charged slightly more than some of the other clients, but I know it would be worth every penny. Especially the dance class. It's called Basic Movement. They also offer square dancing and ballet, but I thought she should start out slowly."

"She's not 'starting out' at all. It's a ridiculous idea. You can put that piece of paper in the trash. I don't want to discuss it." Marc threw the *Washington Post* he was holding onto the floor with a slap.

"She's graceful and has good rhythm. You've said that yourself."

"Fine. That doesn't mean she has to do *Swan Lake.*"

"She'd enjoy getting out, meeting others. It would be terrific exercise. Just think about it." Leah faltered a bit on the last words, feeling more than a little queasy.

"Ariana is not to leave this house. Especially not after everything we've been through this week. Do you understand?"

"I would never again take her anywhere without your permission," Leah promised, "but if you did give your permission, I'd drive her to the center. No one would upset her. I'd see to that."

"Ariana isn't going to take dancing lessons."

"It's more than dancing. It's the people, Marc. The longer I know your sister, the more I realize she needs friends."

"She has friends. Me. Mrs. Bright. And, I thought, you."

"Of course we're her friends. You're her family. Mrs. Bright and I are her caregivers. She knows she can count on us, but she still needs a social life!"

Marc glared at her from beneath the black slash of his brows. "My sister is retarded. Or have you forgotten that?"

Leah wished with all her heart that she could take his face between her palms, hold his head in her hands and tell him that she understood. She knew his anger was rooted in pain and resentment—pain that his sister would never be like other girls, resentment that he was left alone to shoulder this overwhelming burden. Anger because he was so conscientious that he'd never break the promises he'd made. Instead she reiterated stubbornly, "She needs friends."

He flung himself back into a leather wing chair. "Drop it, Leah. I don't agree. I can't."

"It's important for Ariana to meet others who operate on her level. As it is, the only people she can compare herself to are you, Mrs. Bright and me. Wouldn't *you* be frustrated if all the people in your life could do everything so much more easily than you? More than once I've found her in tears at the piano. She thinks she should play as well as I do."

"Ariana isn't happy?" Marc's eyes filled with concern.

"She's perfectly happy," Leah hastened to assure him, "but she's also frustrated. I want to give her an opportunity to meet friends who are more like her, that's all." She'd found a chink in his armor. The idea of Ariana's being unhappy struck him hard.

"You never know," Leah added lightly. "They teach ballroom dancing. Maybe Ariana would find a boyfriend and—"

Marc went rigid and his dark eyes flashed. "You have no right to make fun of her that way!"

Leah was dumbfounded. "I wasn't suggesting she start dating, for heaven's sake! All I meant was—"

"My sister is not normal. You can't make her normal." His voice cracked with pain. "You don't understand, Leah. My parents accepted Ariana's limitations. I've accepted them. Now it's your turn."

"But—"

"There are no ifs, ands or buts about it. My word is final. If you can't understand that, then perhaps you aren't cut out to work in this household."

Leah bit her lip in disappointment. She'd gone too far. She was Ariana's only hope for a richer life, and she had failed.

"ARE YOU ALL RIGHT?" Mrs. Bright peered worriedly at Leah. "You aren't catching a cold, are you?"

"I wish it was that simple," Leah muttered.

"Want to talk about it?" Mrs. Bright placed a cookie jar on the counter. "The tea is made and the oatmeal cookies are fresh. Ariana is so engrossed in her video that she won't want us bothering her."

"I had a terrible fight with Marc this morning. I told him that I believed Ariana was lonely and needed to get out more. I suggested that she take dance classes at the Center for the Handicapped. It made him furious."

Mrs. Bright stirred sugar into Leah's tea.

"It's imperative that Ariana have a life of her own, things to be proud of, ways to obtain self-esteem. What if something happened to Marc? Where would that leave Ariana?"

"He realizes that, Leah. I'm sure he does. But your idea is at odds with everything Ariana's parents believed about raising her."

"I think both Ariana and Marc are going to be hurt if he doesn't allow her to develop to her full capacity, whatever that may be." Leah sipped the tea. Her resolve was firm now. Ariana's running away had convinced Leah she was correct. She would just have to show Marc that Ariana could do things he'd never dreamed possible.

At noon, while Ariana was eating, Leah drove to a nearby mall to make two purchases—a pair of walking shorts and a toy microphone.

At six forty-five, Marc was met at the front door by a pair of singers in shorts and sweatshirts, singing and gyrating to the music of a big portable tape player plugged into the foyer wall.

"We're the Bebop Sisters!" Ariana squealed. "Listen!"

Leah gave Marc an apologetic smile before she was swept up into the musical number she and Ariana had been rehearsing. Leah sang and Ariana repeated "bebop-shebop" in time to the music.

She was either going to be fired or given a raise for this performance, Leah decided when they finished. She couldn't tell by the expression on Marc's face which it would be.

Finally he began to clap.

They took a half-dozen theatrical bows before Marc sent Ariana to change for dinner, leaving Leah to face him alone. His expression was pensive as he studied her disheveled appearance.

"If you'd told me, I would never have believed it."

"About the Bebop Sisters, you mean? They were created just this afternoon." Leah pushed her hair out of her eyes, wishing she had a comb. Marc looked so irritatingly well put-together, and she felt as rumpled as an unmade bed.

"No, about the far-reaching incomprehensible ways you've managed to change this household."

"Oh. That."

He took her by the arm and steered her into the living room. "Since you arrived, I've had to put up with funky clothes, ponytails, loud music, runaways, requests for dancing lessons and, most amazing of all, a homegrown rock group." He glared at her, but a glimmer of amusement twinkled in his eyes. "I want you to know, once and for all, you are *not* taking this particular show on the road!"

"Ariana insisted we sing for you. She said it would make you happy after a long day at work."

Marc shrugged out of his jacket and dropped into a chair. "I have no way of predicting what's going to happen when I walk through the front door anymore. That's very disconcerting, you know."

"Sorry. I didn't think it would go quite this far myself. I bought the microphone this afternoon, and I haven't been able to pry it out of Ariana's hand since. Was she right? Did our music make you happy?"

With an exasperated expression, Marc rose and walked toward her. Before he could speak, Ariana entered with Mrs. Bright close behind.

"We can sing pretty, can't we, Marc?" Ariana's eyes were shining, and her smile was so wide it seemed to light the room.

"You sing beautifully, Ariana."

The girl responded by flinging her arms around her brother.

As Marc laid his cheek against his sister's golden head, Leah thought she saw a hint of moisture in his beautiful brown eyes.

WHEN MRS. BRIGHT came into the dining room to clear away the dinner dishes, Marc asked, "Would you see to it that Ariana gets settled upstairs? I want to talk to Leah."

Now what? Leah wondered. She trailed Marc into the living room, watching the movement of his long, muscular legs. She guessed he'd been a runner at some point in his life. He had such an easy stride, such a comfortable way of walking.

As Marc sank into a chair, she noticed how wide his shoulders were. The loud music must have affected her brain, she told herself sharply. She was thinking like an infatuated teenager!

Leah sat across from him, and they stared at each other until she blinked, breaking the intense connection of their eyes. Marc licked his lips and uttered the two words Leah had never expected to hear.

"You win." At her blank look, he explained, "You win. Ariana can go to dance classes at the Center for the Handicapped. If things don't work out—if she's frightened or unhappy in any way—I don't want you to push it. I want her to know that she doesn't have to do anything that upsets her."

"Marc, are you serious?"

"I'm out of my mind." He raked his fingers through his hair, leaving it a tousled but attractive mess. "And I have you to thank for that."

"I'll be with her every minute, Marc, I promise. I'd never let anything happen to Ariana." An idea struck Leah with the force of a two-ton truck. "In fact, I think you should come along the first time to see for yourself that everything will work out."

"You want me to leave my office in the middle of the day to go dancing with my sister?"

"Why not? You'll be worrying about her, anyway. You may as well take some time to assure yourself she's all right. How about it?"

Marc gazed at Leah with something akin to awe. "How do you do it? How do you talk me into these things? First the lessons, now this..."

Leah just shrugged, grinning broadly.

THE CENTER for the Handicapped was a bright, sunny place with vividly painted walls and large uncurtained windows. Cheerful music played over the sound system and the smell of freshly popped corn wafted through the corridors.

Leah moved down the hall between a doubtful Marc and an eager excited Ariana. "Come on, Marc," she coaxed. "Everything will be fine." Ariana was too happy to be reluctant or nervous.

"Here's the dance room. Look, Ariana, there's the rest of the class. And Mrs. Macatee. She'll be helping you." Leah placed Ariana in Mrs. Macatee's capable hands and turned to find Marc sitting on a chair in the corner. His arms were crossed protectively over his chest as if something very precious had just been torn from him. As they watched, Mrs. Macatee led the group through a series of warm-ups and simple dance steps.

"See, it isn't so bad," Leah whispered. "Ariana's smiling."

Leah could feel the tension leaving him. "It's just so damn hard," he revealed. "How am I supposed to know what's right for her?"

"Follow your instincts. You're a sensible, intelligent man. What would you say if Ariana were the sister of one of your clients?"

"I don't love my clients," Marc pointed out matter-of-factly. "I can be clearheaded where they're concerned."

"And I can be clearheaded for you," Leah offered. "If you'll let me."

Marc leaned back in the metal chair, shaking his head until that familiar lock of hair dropped over his brow. "You're really something. I've never met another woman—'' He broke off, his gaze riveted on the dance floor. ''What's going on?''

Ariana was dancing with a thin young man with thick glasses and a mass of brown hair. They looked like bumper cars on a collision course, but both were grinning widely.

''What are they doing?''

''Dancing. Isn't that what we came here for?''

''As couples?'' Marc was clearly furious. ''I don't think—''

Mrs. Macatee strolled up to them, humming the tune being played on the turntable. ''Ariana is doing beautifully. I think she's enjoying herself, don't you?'' She leaned forward and whispered, ''She wanted me to give you a message.''

Marc stiffened. ''What is it?''

''She said to tell her brother to ask Leah to dance. Isn't that sweet?'' Across the room, Ariana gestured to Marc as she trod on her partner's tennis shoes.

''She's a darling girl,'' Mrs. Macatee gushed. ''I'm sure you can't resist her.''

Abruptly Marc pushed away from his chair and grabbed Leah's hand. As he spun her onto the tiled floor, Ariana gave them a satisfied smile, before returning her attention to her partner's feet, which were getting in her way with alarming regularity.

Leah chuckled into the front of Marc's suit and inhaled his spicy after-shave. ''You're a good sport.''

He held her close, and she felt his breath on her cheek, warm and intimate. ''No, I'm not. I feel like a fool.''

''Then why are you doing it?'' Leah tilted back her head to study his clouded eyes.

''Because it pleases Ariana.''

Their bodies brushed as they swayed, first to the left, then to the right. Leah became aware of his jacket's roughness. She tried to suppress her rising desire by forcing herself to concentrate on her feet. Right. Left. One-two-three.

"You're a very good dancer," she murmured against his shoulder.

He swung her in a sudden graceful turn. "Thank you. So are you." When he looked down at her, the clouds in his eyes had vanished.

For a moment Leah forgot that she was dancing to a scratchy record in the small tile-and-concrete gymnasium at the Center for the Handicapped—not exactly the most romantic spot in the world. She was transported to a place of light and beauty where she could enjoy being in Marc's arms, feeling their strength—and their gentleness.

Leah sagged with disappointment when the record stopped. In the awkward silence that followed, they shuffled self-consciously off to the side, while the other dancers hurried across the room to help themselves to the glasses of juice Mrs. Macatee was pouring.

Leah passed a hand over her hair and down her flushed cheek. She longed for the privacy of Marc's home instead of the sterile brightness of the Center's dance floor with its interested spectators—including Ariana. When Leah had recovered her composure, she turned to Marc again. He was sitting with his elbows on his knees, his hands clasped tightly together.

"I can hardly believe it," he said in amazement. "Ariana's having a wonderful time. I didn't realize how gregarious she could be. I've always assumed a situation like this would scare her. It just doesn't make sense. Mother was convinced that if Ariana wasn't sheltered, she'd be hurt."

Leah couldn't leave her thoughts unsaid. "Frankly, Marc, it's clear to me that your mother was loving but misguided. Ariana's been too protected. You see that now, don't you? You see that coming to the center would be good for her?"

Marc's eyes flickered and darkened. She had never seen such sadness in a man's eyes.

"Don't push, Leah. Please don't push."

They lapsed into an uneasy silence until Mrs. Macatee approached them, all good-natured briskness.

"Mr. Adams," she said, " why don't you and Ariana follow our director, Mr. Orenson, on a tour of the facility?" Mrs. Macatee beamed beatifically at Marc. He scowled so blackly that he would have frightened away a fainter heart. When scowling didn't work, he visibly resigned himself to an obligatory tour.

"Coming?" he asked Leah through gritted teeth.

"I've been here before. You and Ariana go ahead." Leah cheerfully waved them off, knowing Marc would soften as soon as Ariana's natural exuberance took over.

When they'd gone, Mrs. Macatee perched on the chair next to Leah's. "What a lovely girl! She'll be a real asset to our group. So much personality."

"I just hope she can convince her brother that she'd like to return. He's rather overprotective."

"That's common in cases like this," Mrs. Macatee said agreeably. "It's difficult to allow any child to grow up and make her own mistakes, suffer her own hurts. It's a hundred times harder when the child has any sort of disability. But that's still what has to be done." A note of despair entered her voice. "It breaks my heart to think we might not be here to help families through this sort of thing."

"What do you mean, 'not be here'?"

"You haven't heard? About the lawsuit, I mean? I thought you were aware of our crisis." Mrs. Macatee took off her glasses and buffed them with the hem of her skirt. Her eyes were moist and sad.

"The financial problems of the center are bad enough, but we've been making do. The board decided that the center could only pay its own way by opening a day-care facility for handicapped children. The fees would help support all our programs. We thought it was a fine idea until the lawsuit came up." She shook her head mournfully. "When we decided to expand our services to younger handicapped children, we knew we needed a playground area. Since there was plenty of room behind the building, we simply went ahead with the project.''

Leah remembered seeing the newly installed playground equipment, painted in vibrant colors.

"We'd spent a great deal of our funds preparing to take in younger clients. Not just the playground, but furnishing a game room, hiring extra help—and then the trouble began.''

Leah's attentive posture must have encouraged Mrs. Macatee to continue. "Apparently many of the people in the apartment buildings around us believe that a playground and groups of young children would be too noisy. They got together and hired a lawyer. They say the operation of a playground area is a public nuisance. They say that we'll be a disruption around here.'' Mrs. Macatee's chin trembled. "I think they've been looking for some way to get the center out of this area because they see us as a blight on the neighborhood.''

"A blight? This place is beautifully maintained, clean—''

"Don't you see? They don't want a bunch of retarded and handicapped kids marring the neighborhood! Some people are afraid of our clients, others are simply repelled. Much as I hate to say it, we don't live in a very enlightened society, Ms. Brock.''

A slow angry burn started deep within Leah at the injustice of it all. "But handicapped people don't hurt anybody!''

"You know that and I know that, but there are many who don't. It's as though they're afraid they might catch something from the handicapped or be tainted by touching them. It breaks my heart. The people I work with at the center are some of the sweetest, most loving individuals in the world. Now, if the lawsuit is successful, we might lose this location entirely. If so, we certainly don't have the funds to start again somewhere else.''

"That's appalling! What does your attorney say about all this?''

"That's another problem. We haven't got a lot of money for legal fees. We're hoping to get some sort of legal aid....''

"So you don't have a particular attorney?''

"Not at the moment. Mr. Orenson is working on that. We did talk to one gentleman, but he was a rather...cold man. If we're going to have a chance at winning, we have to find a man with real compassion for the handicapped.''

The proverbial light bulb came to life in Leah's brain. She gathered Mrs. Macatee's hands into her own and gave them a comforting squeeze. "Don't you worry about a thing. I'm absolutely positive things are going to work out. Just you wait and see.''

Leah could hardly contain herself until Ariana and Marc returned from their tour. When they arrived, Ariana was humming, her face aglow. Even Marc, who'd looked like a storm cloud when he'd left, wore a satisfied expression.

After they climbed into the car, Ariana dozed off, her head resting against a pillow made of Marc's costly tweed jacket. Leah decided this was the perfect time to approach him with the center's problems.

"Well, what do you think?" she asked.

"About what?" His voice was vague, distant, which didn't bode well for what Leah had to say next.

"The center, of course! Did you like it?"

"It was all right, I suppose." He stared at the windshield as if mesmerized by the car ahead of him.

"Ariana loves it. She's very happy there."

"Perhaps."

She knew he was being stubborn and obtuse just to fluster her. Well, she wasn't going to let him get away with that. "Ariana is enchanted with the center. You'd have to be blind not to see it!"

"Maybe."

"It's unfortunate that something she enjoys so much might be taken away from her."

"I didn't say she had to quit going . . . yet."

"I mean the center itself. It might have to close. Over a stupid lawsuit." Now she had him interested. Leah licked her lower lip. "Mrs. Macatee told me about it." Leah poured out the story of the irate neighbors and their vision of a "public nuisance" somehow polluting their neighborhood. As she spoke, Marc's grip on the steering wheel tightened until his knuckles turned white.

"That's absolutely ridiculous!" he finally blurted. "Children in a playground, especially supervised handicapped children aren't a nuisance."

"I know that, but apparently the neighborhood group has organized a large protest to stop the expansion—" she paused theatrically "—and the center doesn't even have an attorney."

Marc's head twisted sharply. "Oh, no, you don't. You're not going to get me involved in this. I've got more on my plate than I can handle now. Besides, I'm not even sure I approve of the center, at least not for Ariana. She'd be just as well off at home, in my opinion."

"At least think of the others, then! Those people need an outlet. A place to go and meet friends. Marc, you could take care of that awful committee in no time at all!"

"Thanks for the vote of confidence." His lips quirked in a slight smile. "I can see you don't know much about the law."

"No? Perhaps not, but I do know about the handicapped. And I know about you."

She hadn't meant the statement to sound quite so personal, and she certainly hadn't expected the warmth in his eyes. Fortunately—or perhaps unfortunately—Ariana chose that moment to awaken.

"Can I go back to the center tomorrow, Marc? I want to dance."

Leah spread her hands wide and gestured eloquently. "See?"

Grimly Marc lowered his foot on the accelerator. They were home in record time.

CHAPTER SEVEN

THOUGH ARIANA had been almost giddy with excitement after her experience at the center, she slept late the next morning.

"I don't think that child closed her eyes last night," Mrs. Bright said with a frown. "Every time I checked on her she was humming and moving her feet under the blankets."

"Dancing," Leah explained as she poured herself a second cup of coffee. "She had a marvelous time."

"Her mother would have said it was too stimulating."

Leah bit back a reply. True, Ariana had a restless night, but so had she, worrying about Marc's current dark mood—the one he'd acquired yesterday. Perhaps she'd pressed him too hard to take on the center's lawsuit.

"Did Marc leave early today? I didn't hear the car."

"He was gone by 6 a.m. He didn't even have his coffee. Said he had an important meeting." The ring of the telephone punctuated Mrs. Bright's statement.

Leah answered it with, "Adams residence."

"Leah? This is Marc." At the sound of his rich masculine voice, Leah felt a rising and falling sensation in her stomach. "I've forgotten a file I'm going to need shortly—it's on my desk. Would you or Mrs. Bright run it down to my office?"

"You take it, Leah," Mrs. Bright insisted when Leah hung up the phone and explained the situation. "I'd rather not drive in traffic. I'm getting too old for such things. It makes me nervous. Besides, it will do Ariana good to sleep as late as she wants this morning.''

''And disrupt the schedule?'' Leah asked playfully.

''If you can do it, so can I.'' Mrs. Bright jabbed at the oatmeal she had simmering on the stove. ''Run along. No need to hurry back.''

Feeling like a child playing hooky, Leah took the stairs two at a time. Once in her room, she slipped out of the simple skirt and blouse she was wearing and plucked a pale blue linen suit from the closet.

''City clothes!'' Leah exclaimed gleefully, remembering the evening Melanie Dean had come to the house. She refused to play the part of the lowly servant today. She dressed quickly, pulled her cloud of blond hair into an unruly but attractive twist and slicked a layer of gloss across her lips. In five minutes, she was in her car, feeling optimistic and carefree.

She refused to think about why it was so important for her to be with Marc. Instead she hummed the tune they'd danced together at the center.

Parking was difficult, and Leah was rushing by the time she reached Marc's building. Her breath was still coming in short gasps as the secretary directed her to his door. Suddenly Melanie Dean glided out of his office, her arms full of files. ''You!''

Leah would have felt more warmly welcomed by an avalanche of ice cubes. Melanie was dressed in a severe black suit with a peplum that accentuated her tiny waist. She wore elegant gold jewelry, and her long nails were flawlessly manicured. Leah felt that her blue suit looked cheap and gaudy by comparison.

''Marc...I...he called.'' When Melanie only glared, Leah squeezed by her. With the heel of her shoe, she nudged the door to Marc's office so that it closed in Melanie's face.

Marc's welcome was far more enthusiastic. "Thanks, Leah! I really appreciate your bringing this down. Have a seat. I'll ask someone to bring you a cup of coffee."

Leah studied Marc's office as he busied himself with the material from the file. One wall was lined with civic awards and citations and another with legal certificates. A third was decorated with artwork, each piece of which cost more, Leah was sure, than she could earn in a year.

Her self-confidence wavered. How could she ever have imagined that she knew what was better for his sister than he did? He was well educated, respected, competent. Where had she found the courage—or foolhardiness—to badger him about what was best for his own family? Her mouth suddenly felt dry.

"Marc, you might want to see these case files. There may be something in them that you can use on the—" Melanie Dean burst through the door in a flurry, her dark hair shimmering at her shoulders. "Oh," she said, not concealing her disappointment, "you're still here."

Instinct told Leah that Ms. Dean had forced her way into the office on a trumped-up emergency. What had she expected? Marc Adams and the nanny in a clinch?

"That can wait, Melanie." Marc tapped the papers before him with the tip of his pen. "Ms. Brock and I have some things to discuss before Mr. Barthold arrives." A cross expression appeared on Melanie's face, but she retreated, obviously irritated by the rebuff.

Being in his office made Leah even more aware of the disparities between them. Marc was her opposite. He was rich; she was barely making ends meet. He was raven-haired and bronzed; she was all golden hair and pale. He thrived on order and schedules; she relished spontaneity and the unexpected. They were like night and day, winter and summer, north and south.

And opposites attract.

Marc's speaker phone buzzed and his secretary's voice crackled onto the line. "Mr. Barthold just called. He's experienced some mechanical difficulties with his car. Would you be willing to see him in an hour or two?"

"Very well. Tell him to meet me here at one o'clock." He punched the privacy button. "Looks like I have a couple hours to spare."

"I'll go home so you can work." Leah stood, self-consciously smoothing the wrinkles from her skirt.

"Why don't you stay here and have an early lunch with me instead?" Marc surprised her by asking. "There's a quiet place just around the corner."

She would have eaten peanut butter and crackers on the White House lawn if he'd asked, Leah thought as they entered the shadowed interior of the bistro. It was becoming more and more difficult for her to separate her attraction to Marc from her position as Ariana's nanny. The entire situation was unsettling. A nanny in love with her employer was a woman headed for trouble. But Leah didn't know how to prevent it from happening.

The waitress brought ice water and took their orders before Leah ventured a question. "Are you sure you can spare the time for this? You seemed awfully busy. Ms. Dean . . ."

"I like the idea of having lunch with a beautiful woman." His intense, lingering gaze made her shiver.

"Stop that!" The words slipped out unbidden. Leah clamped her hand over her mouth.

"Stop what?"

"Oh, nothing." Leah blushed a deep red. "You were looking at me, and I . . ."

"You don't like to be looked at?" He was clearly amused; she could tell not only from his tone but from the dimple that appeared in his cheek. He aligned his knife and fork with the edge of his place mat. "I *like* looking at you."

"Marc, you shouldn't . . . I mean we couldn't . . . If I weren't . . ."

"Does this have to do with my being your employer?"

Leah nodded woodenly. "Things aren't working out quite as I had anticipated." She made a gesture that encompassed the room. "I never expected to be having lunch with you, or dancing with you, or..."

Or falling in love with you.

"We're adults, Leah," he said like a lawyer presenting irrefutable evidence. "We can do as we wish. But just so you know that I understand, I certainly got more than I bargained with you, too."

He pried her fingers loose from the water glass she was clutching and massaged each one. "You're more like a force of nature than an employee, Leah. You came into the house and immediately started turning things upside down."

"Sorry. I do have a nasty tendency to speak my mind." She relished the feel of his hand on hers, gently kneading her tension away. Leah wished he'd never let go.

"It's rather unsettling, you know. There's always a grain of wisdom in what you say that prevents me from dismissing your ideas."

"I'm sorry to be so much trouble, Marc, but I truly care about your sister."

"I know that. I see it every day." He ran his tongue along his lower lip. Leah followed the movement raptly, her stomach tightening with desire.

"Irritating as you are, Leah, you do have a certain...appeal." He said the word so tenderly it seemed like a caress.

"Thank you. I think." Leah was acutely conscious of their hands touching again.

"Much as I hate to admit it, before you arrived we'd become a bit...staid. You're the catalyst bringing us back to life."

"I was afraid you were angry with me."

"I have been angry and no doubt will be again." He searched her face, his gaze purposeful and intent. "But one good thing you've done is shaken us—me—out of mourning. Nothing will bring my parents back, relieve the burden of my sister from my shoulders or make my life more serene. I see that now."

His words made Leah feel bold enough to broach a risky subject. "Marc, I've been thinking about that lawsuit against the center. Could it really put the place in jeopardy?"

He paused thoughtfully before answering. "I believe it could, if the facts are as you've stated. I hope they have a charitable attorney who's willing to be patient about payment."

"But that's the problem, Marc! The center doesn't even *have* an attorney. After all, it's a relatively small private facility. They're floundering around not knowing what to do next."

"They'd better find some legal help—soon."

Leah gave him her most beguiling look. "Could you do it, Marc? Could you help them with the lawsuit?"

He stared at her as if she'd asked him to put his sports car through the trash compactor. "When would I find time to do gratis work for that organization? I'm not even sure my sister should be going there."

"But, Marc, surely you could see how much more confident Ariana was after only one visit. How happy... It would be awful to take that away from her now that she's making new friends."

"No way." The stubborn thrust of his chin and the narrowing of his dark eyes told Leah he'd dug in his heels and was not about to budge on the issue.

"I think you're being unfair."

"Me?" Marc gazed at her in disbelief. "What have I done?"

"Even if you don't think the center is the right place for Ariana, think of all those others who were having such a wonderful time! Think of the younger children who would benefit from a place like that. Can you deny all of them just because you have some silly hang-up about your sister being in a place like that?''

"I'm not denying anyone—''

"Think of the parents of those handicapped children! Not everyone can afford a nanny, Marc. Some of those parents worry every day about what kind of care their children are getting. The center is a lifesaver for dozens of families who can't afford people to come into their homes.''

"Come on, Leah, don't be so dramatic. They'll find a lawyer—''

"Not one as good as you.''

"You don't know what kind of lawyer I am. Maybe I'm lousy.''

"Do you expect me to believe that?''

A telltale grin quirked at the corner of his mouth. "Okay, so I'm a good attorney. That doesn't mean I have time to offer my services to the center.''

"Just look into it. See what's happening, what can be done. Think about Ariana, or at least the people like her who aren't lucky enough to have a nanny and a housekeeper!''

"I could investigate a little, I suppose, and recommend someone who might help them.''

"That would be wonderful, Marc! Thank you, thank you, thank you!'' Leah grasped his hands and gave him a wide smile. "I knew you were a good man.''

"It's not that simple, Leah. This isn't a case of good versus bad.''

Leah ignored his skepticism. At least he'd look into the center's problems, and that was a step in the right direction.

They finished their meal, making companionable small talk about favorite books and movies. When the waitress brought the bill, both were surprised at how quickly the time had passed.

"If I don't leave now, I'm going to miss my client again," Marc said, dropping his napkin on the table.

"And I'm taking advantage of Mrs. Bright."

"Next time, I won't have a client waiting for me at the office," he promised.

Next time?

"Will you have dinner with me one night, Leah?"

She nodded and said, "Yes," her voice soft and tremulous.

They rose in unison, with the scraping of chair legs against the restaurant's scrubbed pine floor. As Leah leaned over to retrieve her purse she lost her balance. Marc steadied her, but didn't immediately release her arms. She heard his quick intake of breath and felt his face very near her own.

"Marc, I . . ." He silenced her with a kiss. Her parted lips were soft and pliant beneath his. Her breath grew shallow, her pulse quick, her body warm.

The flame died as quickly as it had flared. They both seemed to recover their senses at once.

Leah stumbled backward, stammering nonsense about getting home, acutely aware of the smirking waitress and a table of interested diners. Marc, deeply flushed beneath his tan, made a show of straightening his tie. They spoke simultaneously.

"I shouldn't have done that . . ."

"I normally don't . . ."

"I'm sorry, Leah. I had no right to do that—not now, or the night Ariana was lost, either." Marc flung cash onto the tray that held their bill. "Sometimes with you, I . . . forget."

"Forget?" Leah's voice was ragged.

"Forget our relationship. Forget that you've come to my home for Ariana. Not for me." His expression grew stony. "I apologize. It won't happen again."

Leah was struck by a bleak sense of hopelessness, of futility. Would there ever be more for them than this?

"TONIGHT? YES, I FORGOT. I've had a lot on my mind lately... You know I don't like these things, but okay... I'll arrange my own, thank you... Nine... Yes, yes, I know. See you then."

Leah listened curiously to Marc's one-sided conversation. He was speaking on the kitchen phone, and she couldn't help overhearing. Just as she started for the stairs, he grabbed her by the arm.

"Wait, Leah, I need your help—again."

"Sure. Name it. Is there some sort of emergency?"

"You might say that." He appeared amused at the idea. "Ted Forester is having a party."

"That *is* an emergency."

"Don't be sarcastic. You don't understand Ted."

"I don't even *know* Ted. Marc, what's going on?"

"Ted Forester is one of my law partners. He's having a party tonight and insists I come. I usually turn him down, but it's becoming difficult not to offend him."

"Doesn't sound all that horrible to me," Leah said bluntly as she extricated herself from Marc's grip. "I haven't been to a party in ages. Why don't you go for half an hour, eat a plate of food and leave?"

"It's not that easy with Ted. Besides, I've neglected my social obligations lately." He studied Leah speculatively. "Of course, if you came with me and happened to suffer a debilitating headache soon after our arrival..."

Leah held up her hand. "Oh, no, you don't! I'm not going to be your excuse. I'm a nanny, remember? Ariana's nanny, not yours."

He had the grace to look embarrassed. "I just thought if you came along we could leave a little earlier." He glanced at her slyly. "Besides, I already told him I'd be bringing a date."

Leah felt the trap he'd set for her snap shut. She was half flattered, half frustrated.

"Oh, I suppose. Do I get a bonus for work above and beyond the call of duty?"

"We'll leave here in forty-five minutes." Marc's grin was triumphant. "Ted said to bring a bathing suit."

Leah was still wondering how Marc had talked her into this as he knocked at the door of a lovely English tudor home on the far side of Bethesda. The small tote she clutched held a daring two-piece suit, the one she usually reserved for private sun bathing. But she was definitely having second thoughts about letting Marc see her in the suit her brothers had once cheerfully labeled obscene.

"There you are!" A loud friendly voice boomed from the doorway. "I thought you were going to worm out of this and... Well, well, who have we here? Your date? And very lovely, too. It's about time, Marc."

They were drawn into the house by a tall, gaunt-looking man in his mid-thirties. He bordered on ugly until he smiled. Then, revealing dancing blue eyes and a mouthful of crooked teeth, he reminded Leah of a gleeful Halloween goblin. She liked him immediately.

"Hiya. I'm Ted Forester—Marc's partner. One of them. The smart one." He winked naughtily. "Obviously no one ever hires me for my looks."

"Don't let this guy fool you, Leah," Marc said, stepping in to rescue her. "I hired him for comic relief."

Ted shooed them toward the back of the house. As they moved through the rooms, Leah got a glimpse of cozy masculine furnishings, books and clutter. There was a delectable smell wafting from the kitchen.

"I've been cooking ribs, chicken wings, stuffed mushrooms—you know, finger food." Ted pointed to a laden table. "Help yourself."

There were three other couples clustered around the table sampling the food and praising it loudly. They all turned to watch Marc and Leah enter.

Briskly Marc introduced Leah to Frank Grant, his other partner, Jerry Weber, the office manager, and Harry Morley, the accountant as well as Harry's wife, Linda. Frank's and Jerry's dates introduced themselves.

"Eat up, make yourself comfortable, take a dip—the hot tubs are all bubbling," Ted invited. His own date was a lovely redhead named Nita.

After a few minutes of polite conversation the couples began drifting away on their own. Even Ted and Nita seemed unconcerned about their roles as host and hostess. Ted was too busy feeding Nita bites of French bread dipped in warm cheddar sauce.

"Now what?" Leah whispered, feeling out of place.

"Let's join the others. I think Frank and Jerry would like to get to know you. I seldom bring a date to any social function I attend, and if it isn't tied to business in some way, I rarely bother to go. The quicker we satisfy their curiosity, the sooner we can leave."

The back of the house opened onto a huge private garden with an open fireplace, a bubbling hot tub big enough for eight, and multiple strings of Japanese lanterns.

When Marc went to get them drinks, Jerry Weber sauntered up to Leah. "Ted throws a great party, doesn't he? Too bad Marc hardly ever comes. Maybe you can do something about that. He seems to think if he can't woo a client at a party, it's not worth attending. He's no fun at all anymore."

Leah was at a loss for words. Marc's friends and associates weren't at all what she expected—a pack of men dressed like penguins, standing around discussing the finer points of the law, not the relaxed festive bunch she found here.

Marc's arrival at her side saved her from having to respond to Jerry. He led her into the living room, where they sank into one of the plush leather couches, balancing their drinks and plates of food. "Ted must spend ten percent of his salary on candles," Marc mused.

"Your friends are very...nice."

Marc chuckled. "Very different from me, you mean."

"That, too."

He stared at a distant spot somewhere over Leah's head. "I used to be more like them, before..."

"You don't have to cut yourself off from your friends in order to care for Ariana, you know," she told him gently.

"I realize that. It's just that I feel so much more responsibility now." He gave a lopsided little grin. "Besides, I never enjoyed parties."

A shrill giggle from the hot-tub area off the patio caught their attention.

"Care to take a dip when we've finished eating?" Marc asked. "After that, I think we can sneak out without any repercussions."

Leah was thankful to find an entire row of fluffy white terry robes hanging in the bathroom. She slipped out of her clothes and into the bikini. Marc met her in the hallway. He, too, wore one of the robes. Instead of cinching it tightly around himself, he'd let it hang open, giving Leah a glimpse of his broad muscular chest.

Together they walked toward the patio, but as they reached the French doors, a groan of dismay escaped Marc's lips. "Uh-oh." He stopped her before she could step through the door. "I don't think you'll want to do this."

Ted and Nita were curled together on a lawn chair while the rest lazed in the hot tub. "What's wrong with... Oh." Around the sides of the tub hung several pairs of swimming trunks and pieces of bathing suits.

"I may have to work with these guys, but there's no way I'm going to take a bath with them," Marc asserted. "Follow me." Leah's heart raced as Marc strode into Ted's bedroom.

He continued past the bed and onto a private patio. It was dimmer here, the only brightness coming from the lanterns on the the wall that divided it from the main patio and from four votive candles shimmering on a small table. Leah nearly fell into the second hot tub before she saw it.

By the time she got her balance, Marc had already shrugged out of his robe and slid into the water. "Want to join me?"

Thankful for the darkness that hid her blush—and what her bathing suit revealed—Leah dropped her robe and stepped into the tub. The water was warm and bubbly, scented with jasmine. Giving a sigh of bliss, Leah lowered herself beneath the surface. "Now, this is better... Oh!" Her toe had connected with Marc's leg. She could feel the firm smooth line of muscle and jerked her foot back.

"I don't bite, you know." His voice was low, barely audible over the lapping of the water.

"I'm not sure we should be here, Marc. After all, I'm just..."

"Shh. Don't worry." He moved behind Leah and grasped her shoulders, gently pressing his thumbs into the tightness at the base of her neck. Leah began to relax.

"That feels wonderful."

"Good. You were looking rather tense."

"Me? I thought you were the one with that reputation."

He chuckled, and Leah felt his laughter wash over her like the jasmine-scented water. His massaging hands caressed her until she was afraid she would melt.

"Marc, I—" She turned to speak, but his lips stopped her. He tasted wet and male and delicious. Without considering the consequences, she leaned toward him.

At that moment, the timer on the hot tub rang. With a start, they both looked up as if expecting to see Ted there, his hand on the switch, laughing mischievously.

"I, uh..."

"Maybe it's time..."

"I really should get dressed..."

Leah scrambled hurriedly from the pool, chased by thoughts of what might have happened if she hadn't been jarred to her senses at that moment. Before Marc could speak, she rushed to the privacy of the bathroom to dress—and to wipe away the tears of frustration and longing that welled up in her eyes.

"C-A-T. CAT. I CAN'T write it." Ariana dropped her pencil onto the table.

"Sure you can. You can write your own name. Cat is a much easier word to learn. Try again." Leah urged the pencil back into Ariana's hand.

"I don't want to write cat," she said stubbornly.

They'd been at this for some time. According to her tutor, Ariana had several words in her writing vocabulary, but getting her to practice them was next to impossible.

"What do you want to write, then?" Leah asked, trying to control her impatience. The fact that she'd caught a cold didn't improve her mood.

"I want to learn new words."

"Oh?" Was this the opening she'd been waiting for? "What words?"

"I can spell Marc, M-a-r-c, but I can't spell Leah."

"You'd like to learn to spell my name?"

Ariana nodded enthusiastically and picked up the pencil.

It was much easier to teach a willing pupil, Leah decided as Ariana worked diligently to master the spelling of Leah. Eventually she began to practice writing her brother's name.

Leah was ready to give Ariana a rest when the girl announced, "I want to learn *another* word!"

"What word would you like? Dog? House?"

Ariana shook her head. "I want to write *love.*"

Leah wasn't completely surprised by the girl's choice. Ariana was one of the most loving people she'd ever known. Sweetness and affection seemed to spring directly from her heart. "Okay, love it is. The first letter is l, which is also the first letter of my name...."

Later, Leah was glad of a respite when Mrs. Bright came to tell her that her roommate, Christina, was on the telephone. She left Ariana still bent over her tablets, working laboriously. When she returned, Leah was amazed to see sheets of paper covered with the words Ariana had been practicing.

LEAH LOVE MARC, pronounced one sheet.

MARC LOVE LEAH, said another.

LOVE LOVE LOVE MARC LEAH.

"Can you read my words?" Ariana asked proudly.

Leah felt herself blushing. "Of course. Very good."

"Read them out loud."

Unwillingly Leah obliged.

Upon hearing the words she'd written, Ariana sat back with a satisfied smile. "Nice," she said, nodding sagely.

"AREN'T YOU OVERDOING this dancing business?" Marc growled a few days later as he pulled on the jacket he'd just discarded. "Ariana has been at the center three times this week."

"I wouldn't ask you to drive us," Leah explained, "but the medicine I've been taking for this cold makes me drowsy. Trouble is, I feel like my head is full of cotton if I don't take it." She tucked a box of tissues under her arm. There had been no reference to the party at Ted's. Leah's cold was the only reminder of the unmentioned evening.

"I'm happy to drive the two of you anywhere. I just don't think Ariana needs to be out of the house quite so much."

The dance class at the center had become a contentious issue between Leah and Marc. The permission he'd given Ariana to go once had turned into twice, then three times, until now she was into her fifth week of classes. Grudgingly Marc had allowed the classes to continue, probably because the joy Ariana derived from them was so apparent. Leah had heard nothing more about the lawsuit and didn't dare ask. She knew how upset Mrs. Macatee became at the idea of the center closing.

"I'm ready, Marc." Ariana drifted down the stairs. She was developing noticeable coordination and grace. Marc looked at his sister, visibly resigned himself to the inevitable and opened the door.

"What's going on at the center today?" he asked as they neared the large brick building. "There're usually parking spaces along here."

"They've added some classes, I suppose." Leah pointed to a spot ahead of them. "Just drop us off over there. We can meet you inside."

"Who are those boys?" Ariana asked, observing three rough-looking young men lounging near the front door.

Leah hugged her purse closer. "Some of the kids that hang out around here seem . . . unsavory."

"Maybe you two shouldn't come down here alone. From now on, take a cab." Marc stopped the car next to the walkway. "I'll park down the street. Be right with you."

Leah and Ariana hadn't gone more than four steps when one of the toughs yelled, "Here comes another one! This place is full of retards. The last one who went in here looked like this." He hunched one shoulder and dragged his leg, cruelly mimicking the halting walk of one of the center participants.

"What's wrong with you, kid?" another boy sneered at Ariana. "Bet you haven't got any brains, either."

"Retards! Retards! Drooling retards!"

Ariana, who'd never been exposed to such language or harassment, turned innocently to Leah. "What's a retard?"

"*You're* a retard!" The older boy, whose hair hung in greasy strings around his shoulders, slapped his palm against his thigh and laughed. "She's so dumb she doesn't even know what she is!"

Leah grabbed Ariana's hand. "Ignore them, honey. They're rude boys who don't have any manners. We won't pay any attention to them. We'll just go into the center—"

"Why are they calling me names?" A note of fear crept into Ariana's voice. One of the boys pulled the skin around his eyes into a caricature of Ariana's almond-shaped eyes and dropped his tongue from his mouth in a lolling drool while his friends laughed.

The laughter didn't last long.

The threesome was so intent on tormenting Ariana and Leah that they didn't hear Marc bearing down on them until he picked two of them up by their scruffy collars and banged their heads together.

Leah pushed Ariana through the door of the center and ran into the fray. "Marc, no!" She flung herself full force against his arm.

Marc's face was flushed a coppery red and thick pulsing cords ran down each side of his neck. "I'm going to kill these little..."

That was exactly what she was afraid of. Once, when she was young, she'd seen a movie of a mother grizzly protecting her cub. She'd always remembered the frenzied, fight-till-I-die look in the bear's eyes, but she'd never seen that look again—until now.

Marc lunged for one of the boys and caught him by the back of his jacket. The terrified boy squirmed so violently that Marc was left holding nothing but the jacket as the boy fell to the sidewalk and scrambled for safety.

Leah clung to Marc, her arms wrapped around his heaving chest, forcing him to watch the boys disappear around a corner.

Marc, his fists clenching and unclenching, his breath ragged, stared after them. "Why'd you stop me, Leah? I would have finished off those little vermin—"

"That's why I stopped you! What good would it have done if you hurt them? What good would that have done Ariana?"

"Ariana!" Marc's eyes glazed and his tone changed to one of panic. "Where is she?"

"Inside." Leah had seen Alf Orenson the center's director, meet her at the door. "I'm sure she's fine."

"You're sure she's fine!" Marc mocked, turning his anger and fear on the only person available. "My sister should never have had to go through this, Leah. I *knew* this garbage about getting out and meeting other people wasn't going to work. I don't know why I ever listened to you." He fought to regain his composure. "My parents were right. This will never happen again."

All the progress they'd made—gone! Leah wiped her hands across her eyes in dismay. Gone because of three stupid, insensitive boys.

"Is everything okay out here?" Alf Orenson pushed open the door. "Ariana told me what happened. I've called the police. They'll want to talk to you. They've promised to put an extra officer on this beat until these ruffians get the idea and leave the area. Ariana will be fine."

"Darn right she'll be fine," Marc said in a cold, flat voice. "She won't be coming back here."

Leah refused to give up so easily. "But what about her dancing class?"

"It was a bad idea to begin with. I'm taking her out."

"What will Ariana say about this?" she demanded.

"Why would she want to come back here after today?"

"She loves the dancing."

"She can dance at home," he said.

"She enjoys the friends she's met."

"We'll be her friends."

"Marc, I don't think it's a good idea to..."

The look he shot her sent Leah back a step. "I hold you responsible for this. I should fire you on the spot, but I know Ariana's going to need you more than ever now. Just don't do *anything* that will put her in a situation like this again!''

Alf Orenson moved close. "Leah is one of the finest people I've ever seen working with the handicapped, Mr. Adams," he said quietly. "I'm glad you have the good sense to see that your sister needs her. But I'm sorry you don't realize that putting fetters on talent and compassion like hers is very wrong—''

"Where's Ariana?" Marc strode into the center, ignoring Orenson's words.

Leah laid a hand on the older man's arm as they followed Marc inside. "Thanks, Alf. I appreciate your kind words. Marc's upset, and he has a right to be. We don't always agree on how his sister should be treated. One of his worst fears was just realized. We'll be able to talk later, when everyone's calmed down.''

In the foyer, the receptionist glanced up and, recognizing both Marc and Leah, pointed toward the gymnasium. "Ariana's in her dancing class.''

"After what just happened? She's dancing?"

"Ariana didn't see you with the boys, Marc." Leah plucked at his sleeve. "She was inside with Alf. She..."

Marc shrugged her hand away and stalked down the corridor.

"Swing your partners, one and all. Then do-si-do around the hall!'' The music in the room was loud and rhythmic; they were having a hoedown. Ariana was in the midst of the flurry, laughing as she tried to follow the instructions.

"She's dancing!" Dumbfounded, Marc stood in the doorway staring at the dance floor. "How? Why?"

"Because she really didn't understand what went on outside," Leah told him softly. "Ariana was alarmed, but she's also very secure in the love you give her. She knew I would take care of her, just as you and Alf would. I doubt the incident had any real effect on her.''

Marc leaned heavily against the concrete wall and continued to watch his sister whirl happily around the floor.

The incident wouldn't harm Ariana, but Leah wasn't nearly so confident about its impact on Marc.

CHAPTER EIGHT

DURING THE NEXT FEW DAYS, the Adams household was a tense, uncomfortable place. Once he was assured that Ariana hadn't been traumatized by the incident at the center, Marc didn't raise the subject again. Nor did he allude to the dinner invitation he'd issued Leah. He'd either forgotten it in the turmoil or chosen not to mention it again. Leah feared the latter. Their relationship had become as fragile as thin ice on a sunny day.

Leah was still determined to help Ariana develop feelings of independence and self-worth. It was more important than ever now that Marc had forbidden Ariana to return to the center. Since it was Mrs. Bright's day off, Leah decided to give Ariana her first independence lesson—making no-bake chocolate cookies.

By five o'clock Leah had realized that melted chocolate was a tactical error. Ariana, fascinated by every step of the procedure, had turned a very quick project into a monumental task. When the last cookie was formed there was chocolate on every surface of the kitchen, except the ceiling.

"Marc will love this!" Ariana gleefully wiped chocolate-coated hands on her chocolate-smeared skirt.

"What will Marc love?" The masculine voice from the doorway was amused. Why did he always look so perfect when she was coming apart at the seams? Leah saw her reflection in the window of the oven door. There was even chocolate in her hair!

She glanced guiltily around the kitchen, amazed at how far two pounds of chocolate could spread. "Ariana, Mrs. Bright will be home to start dinner in half an hour. Go change your clothes while I do something about the mess." Leah wrung out a dishcloth and began to wipe the counter. A stray slip of notepaper caught on the edge of the cloth.

"What's this?" Leah unfolded it. Three words were printed in bold capital letters.

LEAH LOVE MARC.

She was about to crumple it when Marc reached out to pluck the incriminating scrap from her fingers. He arched an eyebrow in surprise as he read it. "Would you like to explain this? Or are you assuming the words speak for themselves?"

Leah felt a blush stain her cheeks. "Ariana asked me to teach her some new words. I—I guess she's been, uh, practicing." She could hear herself stammering but didn't know how to stop.

"What other words did you teach her?"

"None. Just those. Not...not in that order, though." Leah felt like sinking to the floor and crawling under a cupboard. She could practically hear the questions forming in Marc's mind.

With obvious restraint, Marc didn't pursue that line of questioning. Instead he popped one of the cookies into his mouth. "I believe they were worth the destruction. Ariana made these herself?"

"Would I have made chocolate drawings all over the kitchen?"

"I don't know. I never know about you." He carefully rolled up his sleeves and plunged his hands into the soapy water filling the sink. "I'll help you clean up. I've seen Mrs. Bright when her kitchen is defiled. It's not a pretty sight."

As Leah scrubbed the countertop with a vengeance, she was surprised to feel Marc's shoulder against hers. "Taste." He placed a finger on her lip, and she licked it tentatively.

"Want some more?" He picked up the mixing bowl and traced his finger along the rim. When it was thick with chocolate, he slipped it into his mouth. Leah watched him close his eyes and relish the sweetness. "Mmm."

His finger still between his teeth, he gave Leah a slow, lazy smile, which sent pangs of desire shooting through her.

"Now you." He held the bowl toward her. She dipped her thumb into the rich, creamy mixture and raised it, not to her lips, but to his. Leah could feel the silky warmth of his inner lip and the roughness of his tongue as he accepted her offering. She gave a little tug, but he didn't release her. Instead he grasped her wrist and held it steady while he nibbled and teased the tip of her thumb.

"Marc..." She had trouble speaking and seemed to lack the will to pull away.

"Shh. I'm not done yet." Methodically he kissed each finger, then drew his tongue across her palm, toward the wrist. Leah shivered. After placing a gentle kiss on her throbbing pulse point, he released her.

Leah slowly lifted weighted eyelids to gaze at him.

"I'll clean the kitchen with you anytime." His voice was husky with unmistakable desire, and he gathered her tightly in his arms, so tightly she could feel his heart beating against her own. "Oh, Leah, I—"

The garage door slammed like an echo of thunder. "Mrs. Bright!" they exclaimed in unison.

Marc could move quickly for a large man. When Mrs. Bright bustled through the kitchen door he was innocently seated on a kitchen stool, reading the newspaper. Leah, however, was still pink, and her breath still ragged as she clung to the counter's edge trying to regain her equilibrium.

"Sorry I'm late. Dinner will be ready soon. What's this? Cookies?" The housekeeper seemed unaware of what she'd interrupted.

"Ariana made them," Leah said, her mind a muddle. "You'll have to get her recipe."

"Oh, my. Oh, my." Mrs. Bright gazed mistily at the neatly displayed cookies. "I never dreamed it would happen."

"What's wrong, Mrs. Bright?" Marc asked.

"Don't you see, sir? Ariana is...growing up. She's doing things we never thought she could do. Isn't it wonderful?"

Leah backed wordlessly out of the kitchen. She didn't want to hear Marc's answer. Harmony between them was much too precious—especially now. If he didn't agree with Mrs. Bright, Leah would rather not know.

Later that evening, Marc beckoned Leah into the living room doorway.

"Don't you think she's practiced enough?" He inclined his head toward the far corner where strains of "Chopsticks" could be heard. "She hasn't stopped since dinner."

Leah held up her hands helplessly. "I hate to discourage her. It's the first real song she's ever learned. Now that she isn't going to the center anymore, I want to find things to fill her time."

Leah hated herself for giving in to Marc's insistence that Ariana not return to the center. Her desire to please Marc had overshadowed her professional responsibility to Ariana. And who needed a defender more? Marc was perfectly capable of taking care of himself. She'd vowed to work doubly hard to help Ariana gain some independence.

At the mention of the center, Marc's lips tightened with disapproval. He lifted a neatly wrapped package from the foyer table and handed it to Leah. "Dr. Carmichael left these for you at my office. He found some exercise tapes he thought would be appropriate." Marc shook his head in bewilderment. "I never dreamed he'd respond so enthusiastically to your idea."

Leah suppressed the "I told you so" that bubbled inside her; however, she couldn't resist one little dig. "He was in favor of allowing Ariana to attend the center, too." She shrugged and looked up curiously. "Uh, have you heard anything else about the lawsuit?"

"Nothing yet, but..." He paused, as if catching himself. "What makes you think I'd know anything about that?"

"I'd just hoped..." Leah sighed and changed the subject. "Perhaps we'll use a tape tomorrow. Ariana can demonstrate what she's learned when you come home."

Marc put his thumbs to his temples and rotated them slowly. "Fine. It might do me good to come home early. Melanie and I aren't making very satisfactory headway on the case we're working on. I probably need a break—and being around Ariana seems to energize me."

"You love her very much, don't you?"

"I've learned to," he said honestly. "After my divorce, I thought I'd forgotten how to love at all. She's taught me well." Marc leaned against the wall and closed his eyes wearily. Leah longed to stay and massage away the weighty tiredness that settled around him, but unsure of his response, she tiptoed away instead.

Upstairs, Leah sank onto the bed with a heaviness that matched Marc's. *Why me?* She closed her eyes and a single tear escaped to trail down her cheek. Stretching full-length across the bed, she mulled over the knowledge that she loved Marc Adams. This nanny business was more dangerous than she'd ever thought possible.

"ARIANA? LEAH? Are you here?" Marc's voice could just be heard over the pulsing sound of Ariana's exercise video.

He entered the kitchen to find Ariana flapping her arms in time to the music. The legs of her blue leotard were dark with moisture. Leah was on her hands and knees in the doorway of the laundry room, as soapsuds drifted lazily on the floor around her legs.

"What the devil . . . ?"

"See my new tape, Marc?" Ariana asked.

Marc pointed to Leah. "What's going on?"

"I washed clothes," Ariana said as if it were an everyday experience. Then she slapped her hands to her thighs. "I got wet."

"Leah!"

She scrambled backward into the kitchen, mopping up soapsuds as she went. "Yes?"

"Stand up and tell me what's going on here!"

"Can't you wait a couple of minutes? I've almost got this under control—"

"You've got things under control?" Marc demanded. "Is that why I arrive to see my sister dancing in the kitchen in a soaking-wet leotard while you hang that shapely body of yours out the laundry-room door and chase soapsuds?"

Leah settled back on her knees and stared up at him. "Do you really think I'm shapely?"

Marc threw his hands in the air. "Ariana, go change clothes."

Wide-eyed, Ariana obeyed, disappearing up the staircase. Leah threw a bath towel on the floor to soak up more bubbles and water.

"All right, talk." Marc looked grimly at the mess.

"We just had a little . . . accident, that's all," Leah explained calmly. "I thought I'd teach Ariana how to wash clothes. Doing things like this makes her feel capable, you know."

Marc scowled. "We have a housekeeper for that."

"It doesn't matter. What matters is Ariana. Anyway, I showed her how to measure the laundry soap into the tub and run the water before putting the clothes in." Leah gestured to a stack of towels on the table. "It worked fine the first time. Unfortunately Ariana decided that if a little soap worked well, a *lot* would work even better. She used three or four cups. I've never seen a washing machine foam like this one did.''

Marc sank weakly onto a stool. ''What am I going to do with you two?'' he moaned. ''Until you came, our life was well organized and predictable. Never once did I come home to find Ariana tap dancing in a pile of soapsuds.''

Leah gave him a saucy grin. ''Does this mean you're glad I'm here?''

A smile tweaked the corner of his lips, and the dimple in his cheek made a brief appearance. ''I might as well get used to expecting the unexpected,'' he finally acknowledged. ''If I didn't see Ariana blossoming in your presence, you'd be out on your ear.'' His gaze never strayed from her lips, and Leah was sure this scolding wasn't what he was thinking about at all. ''I do presume that you don't have any other surprises up your damp sleeves tonight.''

''Wrong!'' With a flourish Leah gestured toward the kitchen table. ''Ariana cooked supper!''

Marc gaped. The table was neatly set with napkins and candles. ''What happened to Mrs. Bright?''

''She went to the hospital to visit a friend who broke her hip. I told her we'd make dinner. That was all right, wasn't it?''

''Of course, but . . . Ariana?''

Ariana chose that moment to reappear. She was dressed in her jeans, sequined sweatshirt and penny loafers. ''Are you ready to eat, Marc?'' Ariana went to the refrigerator and lifted out a bowl. She carried it carefully across the room to the table and placed it beside a carton of milk. Next, she opened a loaf of bread and placed several slices on a plate.

''There,'' she said as they sat down. ''Eat.''

Marc peered into the bowl. ''Looks great! This is, uh...''

''Tuna fish,'' Leah finished for him. ''Ariana's special recipe.''

"It's got mayonnaise and pickles in it, Marc. I made it myself. Now, you fix a sandwich." Marc had no choice but to spoon out a glob of the tuna and put it between two slices of bread.

Both Ariana and Leah watched him as he bit into the sandwich. Two sets of shoulders sagged in relief when he began to smile.

"It's excellent! My compliments to the chef!"

Ariana, who was presiding over the table like a queen over her court, giggled. "That's me!"

The conversation stayed lighthearted and silly throughout the meal. They finished the tuna fish, half a loaf of bread and two quarts of milk. When dessert—vanilla ice cream—had been served, Leah touched Ariana's arm.

"I think you deserve a rest. You've worked hard today. What would you like for a treat?"

Ariana's eyes sparkled. "Video?"

Leah moved her toward the door. "You may watch a video. Your brother and I will do the dishes."

Ariana turned to stare at Marc. "He does dishes?"

"He does tonight."

When they were alone, Marc put his hands on Leah's shoulders and shook his head with mock severity. "You are absolutely too much for words."

"I just hope the words aren't 'you're fired.'" She tugged gently on his dark striped tie. "We didn't go too far today, did we? It can't hurt her to know how to make tuna salad, can it?"

Marc sighed and moved to the sink. "I don't know anymore, Leah. Ariana's been tested in some difficult ways and come through with flying colors. But I still have this feeling that my parents knew what was best...." His voice faded and he turned back to the dishes.

They worked together silently, and Leah enjoyed the intimate coziness of sharing such a domestic task. She hummed softly as she put away a stack of plates. Suddenly, two very large, very wet hands dropped to the center of her back, followed by two very sensuous lips, nibbling at the tip of her ear.

"Marc, I—"

He silenced her with a kiss. He buried his hands in her billowing cloud of hair and lowered his mouth to hers. Leah knew when he smiled because she felt the edges of his mouth curve upward. She closed her eyes and turned until she felt the countertop press into her back.

There were damp incriminating patches scattered over Leah's shirt when he reluctantly pulled away. She crossed her arms in front of herself. "Should we be doing this? I mean...with our employer-employee relationship and...and everything?" Her hesitant stammering betrayed her true feelings.

Marc studied her face. "You're right. We shouldn't. Not here and not now." He paused long enough for her to register disappointment. "I think it might be a good idea if you and Ariana were to spend a few hours apart."

"No! Marc! We won't do any laundry, Or—"

"Tomorrow, you and I will go out for dinner. How does that sound?"

"Good...fine...wonderful...great!" Leah laughed, giddy with relief. "For a minute you had me scared."

"Wear your best dress. We're going to Shea's."

"AREN'T YOU A SIGHT for sore eyes!" Mrs. Bright's expression was one of admiration as Leah descended the staircase.

"Pretty!" Ariana affirmed.

Leah hadn't felt like this since the night of her Senior prom. That evening she'd made her grand entrance from the second floor of her parents' farmhouse, swathed in girlish blue satin, her hair a mass of ringlets and flowers straight from Betty's Beauty Salon.

Tonight she'd chosen a midnight-blue sheath and pulled her curls into a cascade swept to one side and held with a golden clip. Despite the sophisticated garb, the butterflies in Leah's stomach were the same ones that had fluttered on her long-ago prom night.

Adjusting his tie, Marc came down the stairs behind her. His dark hair, still damp from the shower, lay in perfect orderly waves. As he neared, Leah smelled the heady scent of soap and after-shave.

Though he looked her over hungrily, his words were restrained. "You're very lovely tonight, Leah." Under the pleased, watchful eyes of Ariana and Mrs. Bright, Marc escorted Leah to his car. When they were safely down the driveway out of sight, Marc relaxed visibly.

"Whew! The last time I felt like that was—"

"—the Senior prom!"

"Ancient history. And you managed to make me dredge it up like it was yesterday." He scowled playfully. "How do you do that?"

"I haven't done a thing."

"No, Leah," he said as he maneuvered into a parking space in front of Shea's. "You've done nothing at all—except turn my life upside down." She didn't get a chance to respond, because he was already out of the car and opening her door.

For the most exclusive restaurant in the city, Shea's was surprisingly unassuming. In fact, it didn't even advertise; the right people just knew about it.

The deceptively simple decor was the perfect backdrop for the beauty, power and influence of the people who dined there. Marc requested a table near the wall, secluded yet suitable for stargazing.

"Isn't that the senator who's been in the paper all week?" Leah asked.

Marc, looking slightly bored, only nodded.

"He was on the cover of one of those newsmagazines, too!" Leah poked Marc's wrist. A pixieish expression lit her eyes as she viewed his indifferent pose. "Isn't this exciting? Of course I don't go out much. Everything is exciting to me. Even laundry."

Marc took Leah's hand between his own. The warmth of his palms radiated through her fingers, and soon Leah felt every nerve ending in her body pulse. "Do I dare let you go back to the house?"

"I swear I'll be good. No matter what, I won't teach Ariana to use the chain saw or the blender."

"Thank goodness for small favors. At least my trees are safe." He laughed and the tiredness that so often etched lines in his face suddenly vanished. He spoke as if choosing his words carefully. "I appreciate the affection you have for my sister."

But Marc, it's nothing compared to what I feel for you. Frustration gnawed at Leah. Was that all he could say? Was this beautiful night on the town merely his expression of gratitude? A treat for the poor little nanny who was trapped at home?

Other questions nagged at her. Was Marc genuinely interested in her? Or was he simply rewarding her for being so good with Ariana?

Don't fool yourself into thinking there's hope for you and Marc. You've never indulged in pipe dreams. Don't start now.

Leah ran a fingertip around the rim of her crystal goblet, her eyes downcast.

"You look sad." Marc's eyes were tender and compassionate—the emotions that made her most vulnerable. He played with a stray golden curl that lay on her cheek. "Would you like to go dancing?" he offered, cheering her immediately. "I hear through the grapevine that Scavvi's is a place we shouldn't miss."

He patted his jacket, obviously searching for something. "Now, if I can find my keys, we'll be on our way.... What's this?" He withdrew a folded sheet of lined paper from his pocket. With an amused shake of his head, he thrust the paper at Leah.

MARC LOVE LEAH

As Leah felt embarrassment wash over her, he refolded the note and returned it to his pocket. Ariana! What would she think of next?

LEAH WAS IMPRESSED that Marc had bothered to find out what the city's hottest night spot was. Her toe took on a life of its own, tapping to the beat of the music as they stood in the doorway of Scavvi's viewing a dance floor filled with gyrating couples.

"Remember that high school prom we talked about?" Marc asked lightly. "That was the peak of my dancing career. That, and the afternoon we danced at the center. Do you still want to be here with me?"

More than you could possibly know.

When he swung her onto the dance floor, his movements were strong and unfaltering. Leah fell into step with him easily, as if they'd been dancing together all their lives.

"Want a drink? Anything? All we've done is dance." He placed his cheek atop her glossy blond head and caressed her shoulder with his thumbs.

"No." Leah savored the feel of his fragrant warm shirt against her skin and smiled. "Everything is just perfect."

"You smell like peaches," he murmured as his lips skimmed her hair. It seemed natural for Marc to lower his head and catch her lips with his own. The first kiss was tentative and inquiring, the second more intense, more exciting. Marc rested his hands on the gentle curve of her hips and drew her toward him. It took them long, languorous moments to realize the music had ceased.

Leah stared about her, dazed. "We seem to be the last ones on the dance floor."

Marc's chuckle so close to her ear brought gooseflesh to her slender arms. "Maybe we should go home." He looked at her speculatively. "And finish what we've started."

Leah knew there was only one "finish" to what she and Marc had started. . . .

She drifted back to the house on a delicious cloud. Marc was silent but, by putting his arm around her, he told her what she needed to know. He cared for her. He wanted her. Tonight. A shiver of nervous anticipation ran through her as they neared the house.

Leah followed Marc to the door. As he slipped his key into the lock, she moved to the smoked-glass window that opened onto the foyer. "I see Mrs. Bright left some lights on. That was sweet. . . ."

On tiptoe, she leaned forward to peer inside.

"Don't touch that!" Marc warned too late.

Leah wavered and tried to steady herself by grabbing the protective wrought-iron grid covering the window. A loud whooping sound filled the air.

He uttered an expletive. "You just triggered the burglar alarm, Leah." He shoved open the door and raced to the study. Within moments, the raucous noise subsided.

Mrs. Bright reached the bottom of the stairs just as Leah entered. "Mr. Marc? Is that you?"

"It's okay. I turned off the switch and called the police to tell them it was a false alarm."

"I was sure I only turned on one alarm," Mrs. Bright said. "Why . . . ?"

"Leah tripped it." Marc told her. "I don't think she realized the doors and windows in this house are wired separately." To Leah he explained, "When she goes to bed, Mrs. Bright turns on the burglar alarm that's wired to the windows. The doors are connected to a different switch so that when I come home I can get in without disturbing anyone.'' He shook his head. ''I'm sorry. It was a terrible oversight not to tell you.''

Leah silently cringed at her foolishness, wondering if she'd ever live this down.

Mrs. Bright secured her robe around her ample middle. ''Now that I'm up, I'll be glad to make some coffee. How does that sound? There's apple pie. A little snack will help settle everyone's nerves. Otherwise none of us will sleep tonight.''

Marc gave a single longing glance at Leah before turning to the housekeeper. ''You're right. We may as well eat that pie, though I doubt some of us will sleep, anyway.''

CHAPTER NINE

"TOAST? BAGEL? EGGS?"

Leah gazed moodily into the bottom of her mug as Mrs. Bright attempted to ply her with food. Her mind and stomach had been on a roller-coaster ride these past few days. Until she figured out her relationship with Marc, Leah doubted things would improve. Even late-night visits to the ever-understanding Christina hadn't helped Leah sort out her problems.

"Early for calls," Mrs. Bright remarked as the telephone rang. Deftly she slid a perfect omelet onto a plate. "Now here's—"

Before she could finish her sentence Marc burst through the door, his face set in a somber expression. "For you, Leah. You'd better take it in the study."

When Leah returned, her smile was brittle, and she clasped her hands together tightly. "That was my father. My grandmother broke her leg yesterday. Apparently it's quite bad, but the doctor is confident it'll heal properly. They're going to put a pin in the leg today."

"Your father sounded rather shaken to me," Marc commented.

"Dad's squeamish about hospitals." Leah reached for a slice of toast she didn't feel like eating. A wave of homesickness washed over her. "I wish I was closer so I could visit. Gran's furious with herself. She was trying to change a light bulb and fell off the ladder."

"Why don't you go see her?"

Leah stared at him. "In Wisconsin?"

"Why not? Airline connections are good."

"I couldn't. I have a job here. I wouldn't leave you and Mrs. Bright with my responsibilities."

"Nonsense. I'm not suggesting you go permanently. You can fly out today and be back before the weekend is over. We can get along without Leah that long, can't we, Ariana?"

If Marc had hoped for help from that quarter, he didn't get it. Ariana gave him a doubtful look that said she wasn't sure *she* could get along without Leah, even for a day.

"It's wonderful of you to offer, but I couldn't go unless—" a sudden inspiration hit Leah "—unless Ariana would like to come with me!"

"Yes!" Ariana clapped her hands and jumped out of her chair. "Oh, Marc, please!"

"She could meet my cousin Mary and see all the farm animals. My mother would be delighted to have her. Think of the experience!"

"I want to ride in an airplane!" Ariana shot a pleading glance at her older brother.

"Absolutely not." Marc shook his head with quiet determination. "Leah, you know better than to ask. Ariana does not need to visit a farm in Wisconsin—now or ever."

"Then I won't go, either. She's my responsibility."

"That's ridiculous, Leah! I'm giving you the time off."

"And I'm not taking it. My family will do fine without me. I've made a commitment to you and I'm going to keep it." Her chin came out in a determined thrust. She could be as stubborn as Marc Adams! Sooner or later he'd have to loosen the stranglehold he had on his sister and let her get more out of life.

Leah pushed herself away from the table. "Come on, Ariana. Today was the day I promised to teach you a new song."

As they made their way out of the kitchen, Ariana's plaintive voice rang out. "But I wanted to ride on a airplane!"

That night, Leah was reading on her bed when she heard Marc moving down the hallway. His footsteps slowed in front of her door, and after a long pause, he knocked.

"Come in." She hugged her book tightly to her chest and wished she hadn't washed off all her makeup. He strode into the room still looking crisp and businesslike in a three-piece suit.

"I have something for you." He surveyed the ivory and mint-green bedroom, his gaze finally settling on Leah, who was curled self-consciously in the middle of the bed. Without further comment, he tossed an envelope at her.

"Airline tickets?"

"I think you should go to Wisconsin. In fact, as your employer, I order you to go."

"I told you I wouldn't leave Ariana."

"And I told you she couldn't come. Don't be difficult about this, Leah. I know how much you want to see your family."

"It would be a wonderful place for Ariana, Marc. Especially for her first time away from home. Mom would pamper and fuss over her, Mary would love to make a new friend and—"

"I won't hear of it, Leah. I've arranged for Ariana to spend some time at the center while you're gone. You should be pleased about that," he added wryly. "I've also adjusted my schedule so I can drive her there. I want you to enjoy your trip. All right?"

Leah looked longingly at the tickets; she hadn't been home in two years. Marc's gesture was more than generous.

"I'll pick you up at the airport on Sunday." He stroked the tumble of curls near her cheek. "Hurry home, Leah. We'll miss you."

LEAH AWOKE to the smells of coffee brewing and bacon frying. And to the sound of a rooster crowing outside her window. She flung her feet over the side of the bed, reaching for the ragged quilt robe she'd received for her fourteenth birthday. Yawning, she padded downstairs to the kitchen where her father and three brothers were seated around the table.

"You look horrible!" Luke, her usually strong silent brother, said cheerfully. "Don't you ever comb your hair?"

"She looks the same as always," Clayton, her oldest and tallest brother, retorted. "Kinda scrawny."

"If she'd been a fish, I would have thrown her back," Rick, the youngest brother, added. "I thought maybe she'd put on some weight while she was away."

"Or at least learn to comb her hair."

Leah ignored them all. After placing a kiss on the top of her father's balding head, she sleepily poured a cup of coffee and slipped into a chair. The combination of the flight and an evening of chatting with her grandmother had left her weary.

"Why are you guys here so early? I can't imagine you got out of nice warm beds to say hello to me."

"We're helping Dad put a new roof on the machine shed." Luke inclined his head toward the large low building on the far side of the barn. "You wouldn't want to help, would you?"

"Leave her alone, boys," Mrs. Brock interjected. "I'd hoped that after all these years you'd stop teasing your sister."

"What good is she if we can't tease her?" Rick wondered.

"No good at all, far as I can see." Clayton stretched bonelessly to pluck a just-baked muffin out of the basket Mrs. Brock had placed on the table.

"How do your wives put up with you guys?" Leah taunted as she maneuvered the butter out of Clayton's reach. "By using earplugs and blinders?"

"Martha is crazy about me," Clayton announced, refusing to play Leah's game by eating the muffin plain. "Haven't you heard? We're expecting a new baby in the spring."

Leah sprang out of her chair and rounded the table to give her brother a hug. "Congratulations!"

"Hmph!" Rick snorted. "Martha's just crazy bringing another Clayton clone into the world."

That statement brought about a whole new round of bantering. Leah sat back and relaxed, loving the teasing, playful atmosphere. She'd missed that, she realized, living in the stuffy confines of the Adams household.

The conversation jumped and skipped dizzily from one subject to another until Leah's sides ached from laughing. She didn't even think to question why her father and brothers were ignoring the machine-shed roof to visit with her.

"Aren't you going to tell us about your job, Leah?" Luke finally asked, curiosity sparking his green eyes, so similar to Leah's. "And about your boss." Rick and Clayton snickered.

Leah glared at them both. "I don't know what you find amusing. Mr. Adams is a very nice man, an attorney. He's very quiet and I don't see him much. I spend most of my time with his sister."

"Nice, quiet and invisible. Sounds like the perfect boss. Is he old or young?"

"Not old . . . but not young, either. In the middle." Leah was amazed to find herself stumbling over the answer, especially since she knew Marc's age exactly. For some reason she was uncomfortable with her brothers' intense questions.

"Quiet and middle-aged. Balding, too, I suppose."

"With a potbelly?"

"And droopy drawers that don't stay up without suspenders?"

Her brothers were painting a bizarre portrait of Marc, and Leah wasn't sure she wanted to correct it. "What does it matter what he looks like?" she demanded. "Why all the questions?"

All three men suddenly wore such innocent expressions that Leah grew nervous. They were up to something. She hadn't been away from home long enough to forget that those looks were warning signs.

Before she could interrogate them, her mother started to cluck and fuss around her. "Don't you think you should get dressed, Leah? Something pretty?"

"Why? I feel fine. I'll clean up before we go back to the hospital this afternoon."

"That robe is as old as the hills. Go put on a skirt and blouse. You'll feel better."

"I feel fine right now, Mom!" Leah shot her mother a puzzled glance, but Mrs. Brock was staring intently at the clock.

Leah was about to try to get to the bottom of her family's odd behavior when she heard the crunch of tires on gravel outside the window. Luke bent to peer through the glass. "They're here!"

Suddenly the kitchen was a swarm of excitement, with everyone tossing dirty dishes into the sink and picking up stray newspapers.

"Who's here?" Leah was confused. "Who'd cause this kind of excitement...." One glimpse out the window told her what she needed to know. A sporty red car was parked in the driveway and a very familiar male form was climbing out of the driver's seat. "Marc!"

"Your quiet middle-aged boss is here, Leah," Clayton said, rubbing his hands together with glee. "But he doesn't look much like I pictured him."

"How...? Why...?" As Leah watched, Marc, dressed in black casual pants and a red cotton sweater, rounded the car and opened the door on the passenger side. To complete Leah's astonishment, Ariana stepped out.

She was dressed in her blue jeans and a pale pink shirt. On her left shoulder perched a little pair of captain's wings—the souvenir of a first-time flyer. Before she and Marc could walk toward the house, Bosco, the family dog, came bounding up to the car. Unafraid, Ariana laughed and bent down to pet the animal, allowing him to lick her face.

Leah clutched a wad of quilted robe in one hand and a hank of her uncombed hair in the other. *Marc. Here!* No wonder her mother had been encouraging her to get dressed. Even at her worst, she'd never looked this bad in Washington.

She took a step toward the stairs, but it was too late. Leah came face-to-face with Marc at the kitchen door.

"Leah?" He drew his eyebrows together in amazement. "What happened to you?"

"She looks funny!" Ariana giggled. "Messy!"

"What are you doing here?" Leah demanded, taking the offensive.

"Surprise! Surprise!" Ariana grabbed Leah's hand and gave it a squeeze. "Are you surprised, Leah?"

"Obviously," Marc said with a chuckle. "Or she would have combed her hair."

"Leah, are you sure this is your boss? He doesn't look the way you described him." Rick added to Leah's embarrassment, and she didn't know who to strangle first.

Mrs. Brock came to the rescue. "Leah, you go upstairs and put on some clothes while I feed our guests breakfast."

"You knew they were coming? And you didn't tell me?"

"It was supposed to be a surprise. And it worked, didn't it? Shoo. Come down when you're put together."

Before Leah was even halfway up the stairs, her family had surrounded Marc and Ariana, drilling them with questions about Washington and Leah—obviously trying to figure out why she'd misled them.

By the time she'd dressed and pulled her hair into a neat ponytail, Marc and Ariana had polished off their huge meal and completely charmed the entire family, even Luke, who generally took his time deciding about people.

When Leah entered the kitchen, Ariana was staring at Clayton with adoring eyes. "He has cows, Leah! Did you know? He wants me to come and see them."

"So that's the line you use when you want to entice a girl to your place, huh, Clayton? Whatever happened to the old 'come up and see my etchings' ploy?"

Clayton grinned over the top of his coffee mug. "Seems the cows work better. Maybe, if Marc doesn't mind, I'll just take Ariana out to Dad's barn right now. I'll show her the kittens."

From the way Clayton was looking at Ariana, Leah knew the girl had made a conquest.

"Don't worry about them," Leah assured Marc as the kitchen emptied. "Clayton will watch her like a hawk." She glanced around the room to make sure everyone had left. "Whose idea was this, anyway?"

"Ariana's been campaigning to come here ever since the day your father called. Mrs. Bright hinted that Wisconsin was lovely this time of year. And when your mother called—"

"*Mother* called you?"

"She said you were torn between Ariana and your grandmother."

"I didn't know I was that obvious."

"She invited us to come out for a visit while you were here." He was obviously pleased with his surprise. "And here we are."

"Well, I think it's a wonderful idea. Even though you did catch me in such a state."

"Ariana was right. You did look rather funny."

"You don't have to agree so wholeheartedly," Leah chided lightly. She was delighted that he was here in her parents' kitchen, relaxed and tanned and so desirable her mouth almost watered. "Maybe we should check on that brother of mine. He might teach Ariana a few things you don't want her to know."

"What do you mean? Can she get hurt?"

Leah punched him gently in the arm and grinned. "Loosen up. Clayton might get carried away and try to explain the intricacies of artificial insemination or..."

Marc groaned and headed for the door.

By the time they reached the barn, Ariana had been introduced to cows, horses, pigs, cats and even a gaggle of noisy geese. She was sitting on an overturned water tank holding a small gray kitten in her hands. "Look at the baby, Marc!"

"Bad time of year for another batch of kittens," Clayton commented. "Fortunately these are good mousers and it should be easy to find homes for them. You wouldn't want..." He looked expectantly at Marc.

"I don't think so, Clayton," Leah interjected smoothly as a car drove up to the house.

"Come on, Ariana," Clayton said, lifting the kitten from her hands. "Mary's here to meet you."

Marc hung back until Leah took him by the wrist and pulled him into the chattering knot of people. She introduced him to her aunt and uncle. Then she slowly moved toward the young woman who'd been last to leave the car. Leah heard Marc draw a sharp breath. "Marc, I'd like you to meet my cousin Mary."

Mary Brock was the same size and build as Ariana. Her hair, though darker, was similar in style. Even apart from the distinctive Down Syndrome features they shared, Mary and Ariana looked very much alike.

"You're back!" Mary threw herself into Leah's arms with such force that they almost fell over. Once they'd both regained their footing, they turned toward the quietly curious Ariana. "Do you like kittens?" Mary asked. At Ariana's nod, she beckoned. "Come." Without another word, the pair walked toward the barn. Halfway there, in instant camaraderie, they linked hands.

Mrs. Brock laid her hand on Marc's arm as he stared after his sister. "Don't worry. Clayton will look after them and Mary knows our rules. They won't get into any trouble." She smiled gently. "Leah tells me you're very protective of your sister. We're careful of family here, too. She'll be all right."

"Is your entire family that way?" Marc whispered to Leah.

"What way?"

"Able to talk me into anything." He gazed across the farmyard, alarmed. "Now look at Ariana. She's feeding bread to a goose!"

"That's a rite of passage around here. If Goosie Gander will eat bread out of your hand, you're a true friend of ours. She bites everyone else."

"Bites!"

"Hold on, cowboy," Leah said with a laugh. "You can see for yourself that goose isn't about to bite the hand that's feeding him. Relax. With all the people around here ready to pamper Ariana, you should relax and . . . Oh, no!"

Leah stared down the road in dismay as a flashy red-and-gray pickup roared into the yard. The furry dice draped over the rearview mirror were still swaying when the driver jumped out of the truck and planted himself, hands on narrow hips, in front of the milling Brock family.

Luke gave a piercing wolf whistle that made Bosco sit up and take notice. "Look who's finally here! The roof's almost done, Brady. Where ya been all morning?"

"Did you bring a hammer or were you planning to supervise?" Rick wondered.

Brady tugged his baseball cap lower over his brown curls. "I'm helping you with that roof out of the goodness of my heart. You be careful or you might hurt my feelings. I don't work well with my feelings hurt."

"Seems to me you didn't volunteer until you heard Leah was going to be home, Brady," Luke drawled. "Are you sure the only reason you came is your 'good heart'?"

Marc poked Leah in the side. "Who's that? Another relative?"

"Not exactly." Leah closed her eyes and wished Brady Ames would disappear, but he remained standing in the yard as if he owned it, staring intently at her and Marc.

"Aren't you going to say hello, Leah?" Brady asked, his brown eyes skimming Leah's figure appreciatively. "You're looking prettier than ever."

When Leah didn't move, he sauntered over and, with a practiced hand, pulled her close, giving her a kiss that started her brothers cheering. Then, without dropping his arm from Leah's waist, Brady turned to Marc. "Who's this?"

"Brady, this is Marc Adams," Leah blushed hotly, but somehow managed to keep her voice steady. "Marc is my employer."

"Aren't you going to tell him what *I* am?" Brady gave her a proprietary look. "Your boyfriend."

"*Ex*-boyfriend, thank you. One of many, in case you've forgotten," Leah said shortly. Things weren't going quite as she'd planned. Who'd invited Brady Ames to show up here, anyway?

Brady grinned at Marc. "I'm the one she left behind. Hasn't she mentioned me?"

"Brady, stop it!" Leah trod heavily on the toe of his boot. "Behave yourself." The look on Marc's face had her worried. Moreover, she didn't need a clown like Brady Ames ruining her developing relationship with Marc.

"Well, I realize how much fun this is," Leah's father cut in, "but that roof still needs to be finished. Who's helping me?" The men immediately followed Mr. Brock to the shed.

"Marc, where are you going?" Leah blurted when he joined the others.

"To help with the roof." His expression turned mischievous. "I'd like to get acquainted with Brady Ames. And to let him know I'm not going to be ignored as easily as that."

Leah threw her hands in the air and watched him go. "Men! Macho idiots—all of them!" Instead of going to the machine shed, she stomped to the barn, where Mary and Ariana had disappeared.

It didn't take long to find them. The two girls were in the loft, seated side by side on a bale of hay with kittens crawling over them. Ariana giggled as a purring little calico clawed onto her shoulder and stuck its nose in her ear.

"Having fun?" Leah knelt beside the pair. Ariana's glowing eyes answered for her. "If you two don't mind, I'll just lie down here while you play with the kittens."

Leah curled herself into a ball, positioning herself so that a shaft of sunlight from an upper window warmed her face. She watched motes of dust dance through the sunbeam and listened to the girls laugh until her eyes grew heavy.

She might have slept all day if some hay hadn't tickled her nose. Leah swiped at the offending stalk and buried her face in her arms. The tickling moved to her ear. She gave a second irate swat and finally opened her eyes.

"It's about time, sleepyhead." Marc trailed the piece of hay he was holding around the curve of her chin. "I thought you'd sleep forever."

"Ariana and Mary!" Leah struggled to sit up. "They were here a minute ago."

"They were here two hours ago, you mean. They're up at the house helping your mother put the finishing touches on lunch."

"I slept that long?"

"The roof is almost done." Marc dropped to her side.

"I feel like Rip van Winkle. What else happened while I was asleep?"

"Your friend Brady said I worked pretty well for a city slicker."

"He did, did he? When did Brady start talking like a country bumpkin? He's got a degree in agronomy and an MBA. Did he mention that?"

"No, but he said he named his favorite milking cow after you."

"That big dope. I'll get him yet."

Marc smiled and began plucking straw from her hair. "He loves you, you know."

Leah shrugged, falling back against the hay and covering her face with both hands. "I was hoping he'd be over that by now."

"I don't think you're the kind of woman a man gets over easily. *I* wouldn't, anyway."

Leah didn't ask him to explain. Instead she pillowed her head with her arms and looked up into the rafters. "Brady is a very possessive man. He wanted all my attention—or none of it. We dated in high school. When we graduated, he asked me to marry him. He thought we could go to college together and, when we were finished, start a family. Brady assumed a lot of things about me."

Marc's silence allowed her to continue. "Brady didn't understand me. He never has, really. He didn't understand my need to stand on my own—away from family and friends. My need to be independent." She sighed. "I grew up. In some ways, Brady didn't."

"You believe independence is very important, don't you, Leah?" Marc was looking at her with appraising eyes.

"Yes, I do. There are going to be times in my life when I can't depend on anyone but myself. I can't expect a knight in shining armour to rescue me from every problem." For one fleeting moment, Leah wasn't sure if she was talking about herself or about Ariana.

She glanced at Marc, wondering if the same thought had occurred to him. He lay perfectly relaxed on the bale of hay, his eyes closed, a smile playing at the corners of his lips. "What are you thinking about?" Leah demanded, drawing herself onto her elbow to stare at him. "You have a very odd smile on your face."

"Definitions." He paused. "I was wondering exactly what the phrase 'a roll in the hay' means." He opened one eye. "Do you know?"

He pulled her toward him and kissed her. As his firm lips found hers, Leah felt herself melting against him, their arms and legs a tangle on the fragrant hay. Leah cradled his head as he trailed tiny kisses down her neck.

"Hate to break this up, kids, but Ma says dinner's ready."

Marc and Leah separated more quickly than the speed of light, but Clayton's sly grin told them he hadn't missed a thing. He stood above them, mopping his forehead with a red bandanna. "Enjoying a roll in the hay, Leah?"

"So I was right," Marc muttered with amusement.

"You'd better get him inside before Ma sends out a search party." Clayton winked at Marc. "Besides, this guy needs to collect his compliments. Everyone—even Brady—was impressed by the way he works. He's a quick study, Leah. Learned to shingle in no time flat." Clayton held out a hand to help Leah to her feet. "Maybe he'll pass. Tonight will tell."

It was four in the afternoon when Marc managed to get Leah alone to ask her what Clayton's odd "tonight will tell" meant.

"Oh, ignore Clayton. We don't even have to go."

"Go where?"

"My brothers have a little dance band. They're playing for a fund-raiser tonight. One of our neighbors has had several operations and we're having a dance to help him with the medical bills.''

"Maybe I'd *like* to hear your brothers play," Marc pointed out. "Will Brady be there?"

"Undoubtedly."

"Then so will I."

THE HUGE METAL HUT was virtually shaking with music, people and noise when Marc and Leah arrived. Even though Marc wore the most casual clothes he owned, he still looked overdressed compared to the rest of the crowd waiting to enter the building.

"I can't believe I let your mother bring Ariana here tonight," he said as he scanned the throng. "Do you see her?"

"I'd bet next month's paycheck that she and Mary are inside dancing up a storm. You know how Ariana is at the center. If there's music, she's dancing."

"This isn't the center."

As if sent to allay Marc's fears, Mrs. Brock joined them as soon as they walked through the door. "There you are! The girls are having a wonderful time. Ariana's a terrific little dancer." She eyed Marc for a moment before patting him on the arm. "Don't worry about your sister for one minute. I'll watch her carefully. I'm an experienced mother. I raised Leah, didn't I?"

Leah was glad her mother turned away, missing the rueful expression on Marc's face. That was exactly what he was afraid of! Fortunately a few good turns around the dance floor—with Ariana in sight—seemed to relax him. Everything would have been perfect if Brady Ames hadn't decided this was the night he was going to try to win Leah back.

"Do you want me to slug him?" Marc asked after Brady had cut in on them for the fifth time. "My knuckles are itching right now."

"I don't think it would do any good. Brady's built like a punching bag. It's rather flattering, though, to know you're willing to fight for me. I never would have expected it."

Marc's shoulders shook with laughter. "Nothing I've done or seen in the past twenty-four hours is 'expected.' Ariana's running wild with two hundred people about and I'm offering to punch out someone's lights. How did I let this happen?"

"You've relaxed a little, that's all. You've been exposed to the Brock family trademarks—independence, feistiness and persistence."

He sighed as he held her tighter. "The three qualities I've never looked for in a woman, all rolled up into one hard-to-handle package."

She rested her cheek on the front of his shirt and listened to the steady beating of his heart. If only she could stay in his arms forever! The longing was so intense it made her tremble.

"It's time for the butterfly!" Clayton yelped into the mike, shattering the beautiful moment. "Pick your partners."

"Don't look now," Leah had time to mutter before Brady Ames stalked toward them. His dark curls were bouncing and his eyes twinkling as he grabbed Leah by one arm.

"You don't mind if we share her, do you?"

"For the butterfly, Marc," Leah hurried to explain as she saw Marc narrow his eyes dangerously. "First you spin me around on your right arm, then Brady spins me on his left. I dance a figure eight between the two of you. It's a little like a square dance, except the band slowly increases the tempo."

"Then what?" Marc's expression was doubtful.

"Then we're all spinning around so fast we can't see our partner's face and the only goal is to stay upright." Leah shrugged. "I just do it. I don't try to explain it."

At first the pace was slow and decorous. Leah whirled easily between Marc and Brady. As the music picked up, the men's expressions became more determined. Soon Leah felt as though she were on a carnival ride, thrown from one man's arms into the other's and back again. The volume of laughter seemed to increase in proportion to the speed of the music. At the crashing conclusion, Leah released Brady's arm and sent him spinning into the lap of a buxom young lady sitting beside the dance floor.

"Brady doesn't seem to have any inclination to get up," Leah observed, relieved his attention was drawn elsewhere. "Let's get out of here while he's busy." Swiftly they made their way outside.

The stars were white and beautiful against their backdrop of velvety black sky. As they reached the car, Marc stopped and pulled Leah close. "I've always wondered what it would be like to kiss a beautiful woman under a magical sky. And tonight's the night I'll find out."

His lips moved over hers so gently that at first Leah almost believed she was imagining the moment. Then, as his passion grew, she knew that this moment was very real. It seemed as though the world began to move crazily, and all Leah could do was cling to him, the only reality in her spinning universe.

GIDDY AS SHE'D BEEN the night before, on waking Leah felt only exhaustion and a faint depression. It was time to return to Washington. She'd seen her grandmother. She'd visited with friends and family. She'd watched Ariana grow. She'd fallen head over heels in love with Marc. Surely that was enough for one short weekend.

"Bye, sweetie, you come and see us again soon," Mr. Brock said to a teary Ariana. "You make that big brother of yours bring you back."

As the sniffling Ariana nodded, Mr. Brock turned to Marc. "By the way, you and Leah disappeared early last night. You didn't hear the announcement. They earned over five thousand dollars to help cover those medical bills."

"That's great!" Leah exclaimed.

"What's even more interesting, there was one check in the pot for a thousand dollars. There was a company name on the check—Adams, Forester and Grant. You know anything about that?" Mr. Brock stared at Marc. "It's a mighty generous gift. The man who gave it deserves to be thanked."

Marc gave a shrug and a lopsided grin. "If I ever run into those fellows, I'll be sure to pass along the message."

"You do that, son. Yessir, you never know what kind of people might show up at these fund-raisers. Mighty nice ones sometimes."

Marc nodded pleasantly as he helped her father load the car. Leah had to stop working for a moment to rub a fist across her eyes and wipe away a tear.

CHAPTER TEN

THE SPELL CAST by her weekend with Marc lasted for three glorious days. Even Melanie Dean's call on Sunday afternoon about an "emergency" that required immediate attention at the office didn't disturb her. That same emergency demanded his time on Monday and Tuesday evening, as well.

By Wednesday, the magic began to fade. Late that evening, Leah wandered into the kitchen.

"Mr. Marc said he'd heat his own dinner whenever he got home. He works too hard." Mrs. Bright shook her head and scrubbed vigorously at the already spotless countertop. "He needs to take some time off to rest, but that woman won't leave him alone. She phones him at all hours with questions, questions, questions. It's been worse than ever since he took Ariana to Wisconsin."

Melanie Dean *had* begun calling Marc quite frequently. Of course, Leah reminded herself morosely, Melanie worked for Marc—and probably caused him fewer headaches than she herself did.

"Do you want tomorrow off?" Mrs. Bright asked, studying the calendar on the kitchen wall.

"Yes. I have some errands to take care of. I'd also like to check on the renovation progress at the office space I'm renting."

"Do whatever you have to. Don't worry about a thing. It'll be like the old days for Ariana and me." Mrs. Bright took another swipe at the counter. "We'll spend a nice quiet day together."

Mrs. Bright's comforting words echoed in Leah's mind as she went about her business the following afternoon. It was after five by the time Leah returned to the house.

Perhaps Marc would be home early tonight, she thought with pleasurable anticipation. She'd missed their conversations, and the sight of him sitting across from her.

Leah heard the pulsing beat of rock music as she unloaded her packages from the car. As she stepped through the back door, she knew immediately that something was wrong.

The luncheon dishes were still stacked in the sink. The normally spotless counters were unwiped and sticky. In the dining room, a vase of flowers had been overturned and gray, dingy water leaked onto a dainty lace tablecloth.

"Mrs. Bright? Ariana?" Leah followed the sound of the music to its source—in the living room. There, she found Ariana, eyes closed, dancing wildly.

"Ariana? What's going on?" Leah turned off the music and confronted her charge.

Ariana's eyes flew open. "Leah! You came back!" Then she frowned. "Mrs. Bright is mean. I don't like her."

Before Leah could respond to that astounding accusation, Mrs. Bright's agitated voice rang out.

"There you are! I thought you'd never get back. I've been beside myself for hours. This child has been—"

"You're mean," Ariana pointed at the flustered housekeeper. "I don't like you."

Leah, stunned by the outburst, took the girl's hands in her own. "That's a very unkind thing to say. I want you to apologize to Mrs. Bright."

"She *is* mean." Stubbornly Ariana thrust her jaw forward and clamped her lips shut.

"What on earth has been happening here?" Leah demanded.

"All I wanted was to have Ariana follow her schedule," Mrs. Bright said. "You know, do things the way we used to." She dabbed at her eyes. "It might not be as entertaining, but I'm too old for all this excitement."

"Ariana, did you refuse to obey Mrs. Bright?"

"I don't have to listen to her! You can't make me! I hate baby games. I'm a big girl! Baby games are for babies."

"I tried calling you at your apartment," Mrs. Bright was openly sobbing now. "I didn't have any other numbers, so I had to call Mr. Marc at the office."

"You phoned Marc?" Leah had a sudden urge to hide in her closet until Christmas.

"She wouldn't eat, she wouldn't exercise, she wouldn't wear what I asked her to. She even knocked over a flower vase! What would her mother think if she could see her now? The poor woman would be horrified if she knew what had become of her sweet baby daughter."

"I didn't mean to hurt the flowers! Don't tell Marc! Don't tell Marc!" Ariana dissolved into tears just as Marc rushed in.

"What the devil is going on? I got a message that Ariana's out of control." He stood in the doorway, very furious and very formidable.

Ariana flung herself hysterically into his arms. "Mrs. Bright's mean!" she screamed, gesturing toward the older woman. "Tell her she can't make me play baby games!"

Marc glared over Ariana's shoulder, his anger clearly focused on Leah.

"Ariana," Leah said firmly, taking charge of the quickly deteriorating situation, "I want you to calm down. We'll go to your room and I'll help you take a bath. Then you can brush your hair and get ready for supper. You'll have to behave yourself. If you want to be treated like a grown-up, you'll have to act like one. Do you understand?" The sight of Ariana's tearstained cheeks was heartbreaking.

"When you come downstairs, you'll have to apologize to Mrs. Bright. Now, I'm just going to help her clean the kitchen, then I'll be right up. Can you wait for me in your room?" Suddenly the rebelliousness vanished. Ariana nodded obediently and walked toward the stairs.

Leah, aware of Marc's burning gaze, turned to the housekeeper. "I apologize for her behavior today. Ariana is testing her limits. She's realizing that she's not a child anymore, and she wants to be treated like an adult."

"But she's not an adult! She never will be! She's—" Mrs. Bright bit off the word.

"Retarded? Yes, she is. Still, she's trying to see how far her independence will take her. I should have expected something like this." Leah put a comforting arm around the older woman. Her tone was level, reasonable and soothing. "I'll help you clean up the kitchen and the dining room, then you can start dinner. Soup might be nice. Something simple."

"Leah." Marc's voice was icy. "We need to talk about this—after dinner." He turned sharply on his heel and stalked away.

DINNER WAS AN ORDEAL Leah hoped never to repeat. Ariana remained subdued, while Marc sat there rigid with controlled fury and Mrs. Bright snuffled back tears as she served canned soup and crackers.

Ariana ate slowly, without looking at anyone. Leah spooned tasteless broth into her dry mouth and then finally pushed her bowl away.

When Mrs. Bright started to clear the dishes, Ariana, at a nod from Leah, stood up and reached for the housekeeper's hand. "I'm sorry I was bad today. I didn't mean to hurt your feelings." A tear dribbled down her cheek. "Would you help me get ready for bed tonight?"

Mrs. Bright threw her arms around Ariana, enclosing her in a tight hug. "Of course I will, darling. We just had a rotten day, didn't we? Maybe we could read a story or watch a movie. Something you'd like." Ariana and Mrs. Bright disappeared together—the dishes, Marc and Leah all forgotten.

Silently Leah rose to stack the bowls and silverware on a tray. Marc watched her without comment, a thunderous expression darkening his face. He was still frozen in the same position when Leah returned from the kitchen.

"Marc, I . . ." she began, her voice wobbly.

"Into my office, please. Now." He pushed away from the table with such force that the chair overturned with a clatter.

Leah meekly righted it and followed him to the room she was beginning to hate. Every time there was trouble, Marc summoned her here and they cloistered themselves inside. His study had begun to remind her of the principal's office at her grade school. She'd spent plenty of time there, too, always being reprimanded for one scheme or another.

The room was dim and dusky. Marc chose not to open the drapes to the last hopeful rays of daylight. Instead he lowered himself stiffly into his leather chair and propped his elbows on the desk, supporting his forehead with both hands.

Leah sat opposite him, the sweet memory of their time together the past weekend evaporating.

Marc lifted his head to look at her through narrowed eyes. "I hold you fully responsible for what happened here this afternoon," he began coldly. "And I find it appalling. Nothing like this had ever happened in this household before. And it never will again."

"I'm sorry I left today. I had errands to run, and Mrs. Bright said she could handle things. . . ."

"She *could* handle things—before you came. Mrs. Bright is the closest person Ariana's had to a mother for four years, and now, in a few short weeks, they're reduced to having a brawling match in my home." He frowned at her. "What have you done to my sister?"

"I've taught her things she needs to know, nothing more." Leah gazed steadily back, willing Marc to understand.

"Like disobedience? Disrespect? Rudeness?" He flung each word at her angrily.

"She isn't a rude or disobedient girl. She's seeing what the world has in store for her. She likes the taste of independence and wants to discover how far the boundaries stretch, that's all. Children do it all the time."

"You've taught her to rebel against authority."

"I've taught her that sometimes she can make her own choices," Leah retorted. "Ariana has outgrown her schedule, Marc. Mrs. Bright simply didn't realize that!"

He slammed his fist down on the desk with a reverberating thud. He looked so dark and foreboding that Leah shrank back in her chair. "Can't you see what you've done to this household? It's in chaos! All because of you!"

Leah ached for him. The glass wall he'd so carefully built around his sister had shattered, and his safe, familiar world was irreparably altered.

"I realize you're angry with me. I understand that you think I've been allowing Ariana too much independence. I know you believe Ariana should be raised as your mother might have raised her." Leah stood up and reached across the desk to his hand. "But knowing all that, I'm still convinced you're living in a dreamworld, Marc, and you've forced your sister to live in one, as well."

"After what you saw take place today, you can say that? My sweet, gentle sister, who has never before uttered so much as an angry word, stages a showdown with a woman she's known all her life—and you say *I'm* wrong?"

"Mrs. Bright isn't going to be able to work forever, Marc." Leah struggled to remain calm and logical in the face of this storm. "You're a busy man. Shouldn't Ariana develop some of her own resources that will keep her going when neither you nor Mrs. Bright are there for her?''

"I'll be there for her." As he sank lower in his chair, Leah could almost feel his exhaustion and despair. "I have to be. I promised I would."

Leah clasped her hands together tightly to stop them from shaking. She loved this man—this loyal, passionate, caring man. And she had one more thing to say to him before he would no doubt throw her out of his house—and his life.

"Marc, I have another suggestion about Ariana."

"Don't you think you've offered enough suggestions for a while? Although, I can't imagine anything more disruptive than what's already occurred." He raised his arm in an expansive sweeping gesture. "Go ahead. What else do you have in mind?"

"Ariana is seventeen years old. When she turns eighteen, I believe she should be allowed to live in a group home and hold a job."

"What?" He jumped to his feet and held up a hand to prevent Leah from speaking. "No, don't answer that. I heard you the first time, and I don't want to hear it again. That's the most ludicrous suggestion I've ever..." He prowled the room restlessly, occasionally stopping to stare at Leah. "You've gone insane. You're stark raving mad!"

"You might think so, Marc," Leah said patiently, "but I can guarantee that I'm as sane as you are. Saner, perhaps. I'm not carrying any emotional baggage where Ariana is concerned. I can see clearly what she needs. Even Dr. Carmichael said..."

But before Leah could tell Marc that the family doctor had, during their last conversation, wholeheartedly supported her idea, he strode toward her, frowning darkly. "How can you say you care for my sister and still suggest such a thing? Do you know how difficult and painful it would be for Ariana to do that? Do you know how frightened she'd be? How confused? How anxious? I don't know why I thought you cared for her," he raged. "How could I have been so wrong?"

"I love Ariana!" Leah protested, anguished by the implication of his words. "You know that! She's a beautiful, charming girl, and I don't think she should be hidden away from life, from a chance to have friends of her own. Hidden from the opportunity to build self-esteem by having a job and doing it to the best of her abilities."

Marc's unyielding expression made her falter. "But if you don't agree..." She lowered her eyes and asked the question she'd been afraid to voice. "Do you want me to leave?"

He didn't soften or back down. In the past he'd often been willing to listen, however reluctantly, but it was different this time. Leah sensed that immediately.

His answer was a long time in coming. "If you can't see that what you're asking is ridiculous, then..."

Leah's eyes locked with his. "My idea is not ridiculous. I love your sister. All I want is what's best for her. Now if you'll excuse me, I think I should begin packing."

Stop me, Marc! Stop me! she wanted to scream. *Call me back!*

Only silence followed her.

She managed to walk through the study door with her head held high, but as soon as she was out of Marc's sight, it drooped like an unwatered daisy.

As Leah threw clothing into her suitcase, she replayed the argument in her mind. Though she analyzed it over and over, her opinion never varied. She'd done what she believed best for Ariana. Now she'd pay the price and— Her movements slowed as she felt a slip of paper in the pocket of the blouse she was folding. Warily she drew it out, to find exactly what she'd feared, a love note from Ariana—LEAH LOVE MARC.

It wasn't until damp blotches appeared on the blouse that Leah realized she was crying. She wiped the tears away, only to have them replaced by more. As she reached for a tissue, she saw Marc standing in the hall with a yellowed envelope in his hand.

Red-eyed and pale, she stared at him, thrusting the note under a pair of jeans in her suitcase. What did it matter now that her hair was a tangle and her nose the color of a boiled beet. After tonight, Marc Adams would never see her again. Gathering what dignity she could, Leah scraped her hair away from her eyes and raised her chin. "Yes?"

"You look terrible when you cry."

The statement was so unexpected her tears stopped.

Marc sank onto the bed and extended the dog-eared letter. "I want you to read this."

"What is it?" Leah couldn't think straight with him sitting so close to her.

"A letter from my mother. Two years before her death, Mother developed health problems that alarmed her. She decided to put down on paper the concerns she had for Ariana's welfare. 'Just in case,' she told me. What she meant was that if she died, I'd know how to care for my sister."

"I can't read that. It's too private."

"You have to. Otherwise you'll never understand why I feel as I do." He thrust the envelope into her hand. "Please."

Slowly Leah opened it. It was well-worn, as though it had been opened and read many times before. This was Marc's guidebook for Ariana's life, written in his mother's precise and beautiful handwriting. Just looking at the neat margins and the perfectly shaped letters, Leah felt she'd been given a peek at Mrs. Adams's personality. With Marc beside her, Leah read.

The letter was long, detailed and firm. Mrs. Adams left no doubts about what she wanted for her daughter—comfort, security and, most of all, protection.

When Leah finished, there were new tears in her eyes, new heaviness in her heart.

"You've followed her wishes exactly."

"Until the day you arrived." Marc shifted forward on the bed and their bodies inched nearer. Leah's despair ebbed away and was replaced by basic elemental desire. She wanted to hold him, to tell him she understood. But Marc was stiff and restrained, the emotional distance between them vast.

Instead of reaching for him, she continued packing. "I'll leave now," she murmured without looking at Mac. "You can go back to the old ways."

Marc hooked his finger in the waistband of her jeans and pulled her down. She landed, her back against his chest, with a soft thud.

"Don't go."

"I thought that's what you wanted."

"I do...I don't...I don't know." He turned her so that she was sitting in his lap. As she felt his warm breath on her cheek and heard his small contented sigh, the distance suddenly vanished. "You're driving me crazy, Leah. I should have fired you long ago."

"Then why didn't you?"

"Because you're so good with Ariana, and she loves you so much." A wry expression crossed his face. "And because I like seeing you every night at dinner, talking to you...laughing with you. You've shown me how lonely this house had become...." He drifted into a thoughtfulness that excluded her, and Leah didn't move until he spoke again. "The changes are tearing me apart, Leah. Right now this household can't tolerate any more upheaval."

"I'll slow down," Leah volunteered timidly. "I mean, I would, anyway, after seeing how Ariana handled her new-found independence today. She needs time to adjust before she gets any more responsibility."

"*If* we add anything else." She was sure his resolve was weakening; she could feel his muscled body relax.

"Right. *If*. But you do know, don't you, that Ariana could lead a more productive life than she's been allowed to live so far?"

"Don't push it, Leah."

Leah held up her right hand and nodded solemnly. "No more pushing. I promise."

"Then you can stay. If you still want to, that is." He somehow managed to look both doubtful and hopeful at once.

"I want to. There are some very special people in this household. I'd miss them—a lot." Marc lifted her from his lap and deposited her on the bed.

As he rose, Marc ran his fingers through his already rumpled hair, then walked toward the door. He paused and turned to her with a severe glance. "No more trouble, Leah. *None.*"

He was gone.

Leah smoothed the blouse lying in her suitcase. While she unpacked, she would practice the litany Marc had left for her. *No more trouble.* She sighed.

It would be difficult to accomplish.

CHAPTER ELEVEN

AFTER HER TANTRUM, Ariana was quiet and obedient, obviously wary of upsetting everyone again.

Mrs. Bright seemed nervous and fretful as she puttered around the kitchen, often murmuring that she needed "just one more cup of tea."

Marc was silent, brooding and impassive.

Leah felt confident that Ariana would perk up in a matter of time, as would Mrs. Bright. It was Marc who worried her. Even though he'd asked her to stay, something had definitely changed between them. For one thing, he no longer came home for dinner.

Leah wished that it was the center's lawsuit keeping him busy, but he'd given her no reason to believe that.

"I just don't understand it," Mrs. Bright complained one day, a few weeks after the incident. "Mr. Marc *never* used to be away this much. Why, last night I got up at two in the morning and he wasn't home yet. He's going to wear himself out working like that."

Leah wasn't so sure that Marc was spending all his time at the office. Melanie Dean's phone calls had decreased sharply of late. Either she'd given up her pursuit of Marc or, more likely, she and Marc were together.

That idea made Leah unhappier than she cared to admit, even though she held no claim on Marc Adams. He'd never promised her anything. And she had even less reason now to believe there could be a future for them. Their ideas about Ariana were just too different. They disagreed on the fundamental issue that ruled their lives. Ariana had drawn them together—and now was forcing them apart.

"Is that the doorbell?" Mrs. Bright asked.

"I'll get it," Leah offered. "Ariana is so busy with the video game Marc brought home that she won't even talk to me."

Leah hummed cheerfully as she unbolted the door and swung it open. "May I help—" The words caught in her throat as she saw Melanie Dean looking crisp and businesslike on the other side of the threshold.

Without greeting or preamble, Melanie stalked into the house. Her hair was slicked dramatically back from her face and pulled into a bun at the nape of her neck. She wore a dark gray suit with a striking yellow silk blouse. As usual, Leah felt dowdy in comparison, wearing a casual cotton jumpsuit and canvas slip-on shoes.

"May I help you? Did Marc forget something? I could have run it to the office if he'd called...."

"Marc doesn't know I'm here." Melanie cast her gaze around the foyer before making a beeline for the living room. Leah trailed helplessly behind her.

"Then what can we do for you?"

Melanie settled herself on the couch, arranged her skirt to enhance her slender legs and crossed her hands over her knees. "I've come to talk to you."

"Me?" Leah heard a telltale squeak in her voice. "Why?"

"Because you're driving Marc crazy and he doesn't need that kind of aggravation right now. Or ever, for that matter."

"I have no idea what you're talking about, and I hardly think it's appropriate for you to come here and—"

"Oh, don't be so high and mighty. You're just an employee. You seem to have forgotten that." Melanie studied her fingernails casually as she continued. "Employees come and go all the time. I'm surprised you weren't fired long ago."

Leah was so stunned she forgot to sit down. She stood in the middle of the room, her arms hanging limply at her sides, staring at the cool and collected woman before her.

"Frankly this loyalty thing of Marc's is one of his biggest flaws," Melanie said with a sneer that twisted her attractive features. "Once he commits himself to something, he'll go to absurd lengths to make sure it works. That's the only reason I can see for your still being here." Melanie flicked at a piece of invisible lint on the sofa, then shot Leah a venomous look. "That's why I think *you* should see the handwriting on the wall and put an end to this nonsense."

"I'm sorry to appear obtuse," Leah stated calmly, "but I think you'll have to explain what you mean by 'this nonsense.'"

"These silly ideas you have for his sister, of course! Marc's completely distracted by all your wild suggestions about dancing and hairdos and independence."

"He confides in you? About Ariana and me?"

Melanie's eyelids lowered as she perused Leah with an oddly feline expression. "Naturally. Did you ever think otherwise?"

Leah was appalled. It had never occurred to her that Marc might be discussing what went on at home with anyone—especially not the unsympathetic, predatory Melanie Dean!

"Marc's never said—"

"Why should he? You're just the nanny. He doesn't need to tell you anything personal."

"Then why would he talk to a business associate such as yourself?" Leah retorted. "I should think he'd be more discreet."

Momentarily at a loss for words, Melanie made a little sound in her throat that was half purr, half growl. "Marc and I have been working together a lot lately. It doesn't take a psychologist to see that he's finding this situation with his sister very frustrating." She batted her thick black eyelashes and smiled dangerously. "Besides, Marc and I have become very...close."

When Leah didn't respond, Melanie went on. "He was terribly upset about the altercation his sister had with the housekeeper. From what I gather, until you came, Ariana was a very passive sweet child. What have you done? Turned her into some kind of monster?"

It was obvious to Leah that Marc, in his confusion and anger over Ariana's outburst, had talked to Melanie. Melanie in turn, had apparently decided to do battle for Marc. And she wasn't finished.

"He's working too hard already. He doesn't need you adding to his grief. He's the finest attorney I've ever worked with. He's thorough, intelligent and compassionate. He doesn't need to be harassed by his retarded sister and her irresponsible nanny!"

"If Marc feels that way, he should tell me himself."

Melanie gave an unladylike snort and her face grew an ugly mottled pink. "Do you think Marc would be so blunt? That's why I'm here. He's been vague and unproductive ever since you came. Somebody needed to tell you to lay off!" She drew a deep breath and continued, "Marc is one of the most well-respected attorneys in this city, and that's saying a lot. When Marc commits himself to something, he won't back down—even at his own expense."

That was where the promise to his parents fit in, Leah realized. He was a man of his word. Her respect for Marc inched even higher. Leah could understand that kind of person—she was one herself.

In a bizarre way, Melanie was right. Leah knew she *was* causing trouble for Marc. But she didn't want to back down and see Ariana slide back into her safe little world. That forced her to pit her own beliefs and integrity against Marc's. No wonder he was distracted at work, and frustrated with her.

"Besides that," Melanie was saying, "if you continue to stir up trouble, Marc won't be able to concentrate on the case we're working on. There's big money involved, and I don't want to see it flushed down the toilet just because some insolent employee in his household is causing problems."

Leah drew herself up to her full height and looked Melanie directly in the eye. "I'm a professional, Melanie. I've written a thesis on 'mainstreaming' the handicapped. I pride myself on being good with children. I'm creative, inventive and loving. To be perfectly honest, I think Mark has hired himself a terrific nanny. Whatever I do is done in Ariana's best interests."

That set Melanie back on her heels for a moment. Flushed with indignation, she spouted, "Well, Marc deserves some consideration, too!"

"I'm aware of that."

"He's lost enough. First his parents are killed, then he's saddled with a retarded sister—"

"*Saddled?* Is that how you see it?"

"Of course. Nobody would *choose* to be around someone like that!"

Leah mentally counted to ten to keep from exploding. Quietly she said, "I have."

Melanie dismissed that with a wave. "You don't understand. You've got a thing for those people. I certainly don't wish Marc's sister ill. I want her to be happy, but not if she's going to hold Marc back."

"You're in love with him, aren't you?" Leah asked bluntly.

Melanie blinked twice and her face turned a deep brick color. "I, ah, I . . ."

"Does he love you?"

Melanie's eyes narrowed and her voice took on an icy tone. "Not yet, but he will. You can count on it." She gathered her purse and stood up. "It's been a delight talking to you, Ms. Brock. I'll show myself out. Good day."

Leah couldn't move for several moments, her mind whirling with the information Melanie had imparted. Melanie loved Marc. Marc didn't love Melanie—yet. Leah was in the way.

Leah sank to the couch and put her head into her trembling hands. She'd never expected her becoming Ariana's advocate to lead to this. She'd never meant to compete for Marc's affection against a woman as beautiful or brilliant as Melanie.

There was only one small comfort in this whole ridiculous mess. Leah knew something Melanie couldn't, wouldn't, realize. Marc loved Ariana with an intensity that surpassed any feeling he had for his work. And, Leah knew, he wouldn't accept a woman who didn't feel the same way.

LEAH TROD LIGHTLY in the days following Melanie's visit. Though she'd decided to stay and continue helping Ariana, she didn't want to make life any harder for Marc.

Her task was simplified by Marc's frequent absences. Almost every night, he called home to say he was working late and would grab a bite to eat at the office—with Melanie. Though Leah was often awake in the early hours of the morning, she seldom heard him arrive.

In a vain attempt to keep her mind off Marc, Leah threw all her energy into Ariana. She taught her to sew on buttons and hem a skirt, to make her bed and clean out a sink, to play checkers and to braid her hair. Ariana soaked up the attention. They practiced elementary writing and reading, too, and Ariana still wrote her mischievous little notes. Leah even showed her how to make a long-distance telephone call. They called Leah's cousin Mary.

"What are you planning for today?" Mrs. Bright wondered on Thursday morning. "Is there anything left to teach this child, Leah?"

"I thought we might work on money." Leah dumped the contents of her change purse onto the table. "Just in case Ariana goes out one day and decides she'd like a candy bar." Leah pointed at the coins. "Can you sort them into nickles, dimes and quarters? You already know all about pennies."

As Ariana bent happily over the task, Mrs. Bright tugged on Leah's sleeve. "Have you talked to Mr. Marc lately?"

"Not since breakfast a couple of days ago."

"Where is that man?"

"He said he and Melanie Dean were still working on their big case. It should be drawing to a conclusion soon."

Mrs. Bright took the opportunity to grumble, "I don't like that woman. She's too slick for me. I don't know what Mr. Marc sees in her."

"She works for him."

"I hope that's all she does for him. Pardon my bluntness, Leah, but the woman is going to chase him until he catches her, if you get my drift. In my day, ladies didn't behave so forwardly." Mrs. Bright gave Leah a searching look. "I like your type much better. You don't act like such a brazen hussy."

That was the most backhanded, uncomforting compliment Leah had ever received. But, she mused wryly, these days she'd settle for any praise she could get.

Later that afternoon, Leah sat forlornly at the kitchen counter gnawing on an apple. The future was bleak, no doubt about it. And at the moment she felt very much alone. Ariana and Mrs. Bright were both taking naps. The cable had gone out on the television, the mailman had brought no letters from home, the rent had been raised on an office space that wasn't even finished yet, and the man she loved seemed totally consumed with the dramatic and devious Melanie Dean. Leah closed her eyes and massaged the back of her neck. Now what?

"Get your boots on!" Marc stood in the doorway wearing a navy business suit with a battered cowboy hat angled jauntily on his head. "Well, hurry up! Get them on!" He sauntered into the room with an exaggerated rolling gait. "You do have cowboy boots, don't you?"

"Well, yes, but—"

"Go get them."

"I left them on the farm. I didn't think I'd have many opportunities to use them here."

"Tennis shoes, then. They'll be fine for riding."

"Riding what?" Leah asked suspiciously.

"Horses. I have a new client who owns a riding stable. He's invited us over to check out the horses. Want to go?"

Leah stared at him. Not only was he home, unusual in itself, but he'd apparently gone stark raving mad! "Are you an alien inhabiting Marc Adams's body?" She stood up and moved to clutch his lapels. "Where did you put him? Is he hurt? Did you do something terrible to his brain? I've never seen him act like this!"

Marc chuckled, lifting her by the waist and swinging her wildly around the room. "Melanie and I finally finished that case we've been researching. Everything looks very promising. I received two great judgments today, ones I've been holding my breath over. My desk is as clear as it's been in a long time, and the sun is shining. I feel like celebrating!"

"On the back of a horse?"

"Why not? Have you got a better idea?"

Leah laughed out loud. "You're asking a farm girl like me if there's something better than horseback riding? Just let me put on some jeans and I'll be right with you!"

In less than fifteen minutes, they'd both changed clothes and told Mrs. Bright, who'd awakened from her nap at the sound of their voices, that they were leaving. Leah felt giddy as a schoolgirl as they drove to the stables with the windows open and the breeze fluttering their hair.

Capitol Stables was nothing like the dusty stalls Leah remembered back home, places that smelled of horses and hay and fresh air. These stables were groomed and manicured to blinding perfection. The barns, all lining a central courtyard, were colonial in style, with shuttered windows and paved pathways.

"I know people who don't live in houses as nice as this!" Leah whispered as they walked toward one of the barns.

"You'll have to see where they keep the racehorses. That's where they hang the crystal chandeliers."

Leah smiled appreciatively. "I think I'm out of my element here."

Abruptly Marc stopped and turned to face her. "You? Out of your element?"

"Don't tease. I've been feeling that way a lot lately." She didn't mention that he was the source of her insecurity. Fortunately Leah's self-doubt vanished the moment she climbed into the saddle.

"Easy, Nell, darling. Easy, girl," Leah crooned, patting the mare's golden neck. "We're going to have a wonderful ride."

"You sound like you're talking to a child," Marc commented as he mounted a big black horse named, aptly enough, Beauty.

"Horses, children, men—I talk to them all the same. Oops, I didn't mean that quite the way it sounded."

"I know what you meant," Marc said with playful sternness. "More than once I've suspected that you've been humoring me all along. Now I know."

He looked incredibly handsome astride the horse. His strong thighs gripped the saddle and he rode with a straight back and an easy seat. With a little nudge of his heels, he guided his horse onto a trail that led through sun-dappled woods. When they were out of sight of the barns, Leah guided Nell alongside the big black.

"This is wonderful. Thanks for asking me."

"You're welcome. Frankly, when Bob invited me, I wasn't sure I could convince anyone to come. Then I remembered you."

Leah sagged slightly in the saddle. She hadn't been his first choice of riding partner. Who had? Melanie?

He watched her from beneath his lashes. "I didn't mean that as an insult, Leah."

"I didn't take it as one."

"Yes, you did. I saw the way your shoulders drooped." His expression was both amused and apologetic. "I just meant that I felt obligated to check around the office first, but there was no one there who seemed right to go riding with. Only you."

They rode together in companionable silence, the occasional clanking of a bridle and the soft chuffing of the horses their only sounds.

"You look relaxed enough to fall asleep," Marc commented.

"I am relaxed." Leah gave him a grateful smile. "I love this. Thank you." After spending weeks in Marc's huge house, being in the tranquil outdoors seemed to banish Leah's inhibitions. "Ariana would enjoy this."

Marc pressed his lips together in a tight line. "I don't think so."

"Oh, yes! There are wonderful riding programs for kids like her. I'm sure she'd love it."

"No." His voice was as taut and cold as his features. Marc stared straight ahead, his body stiff, unyielding.

"Loosen up, Marc," Leah said boldly. "We're just talking. I'm not packing Ariana off to riding school."

A little of the tension seeped away. "Sorry, I just get so..."

"Overprotective? Someday you've got to realize what you're doing to yourself and to your sister."

"I'm doing my best."

"But your best could be even better! If you'd just consider some of my suggestions..."

"And have my sister accosted outside the center? Or tap dancing in soap bubbles? Or throwing tantrums?" Without thinking he jerked the reins. Beauty tossed his head and took an unwilling sidestep.

"She's also learning how to care for herself. She can mend her clothes and make her bed. She can cook herself a simple meal and clean up the dishes when she's finished. She can call a friend—"

"You're letting her use the telephone?"

"Yes."

"Who's she calling?"

"Friends at the center, my cousin Mary..."

"She's making long-distance calls?"

"We're charging them to my credit card, if that's what's bothering you."

Marc reined in his horse and settled his hands on his thighs, before glaring at Leah. "I'm not pleased about this. Ariana doesn't really need to know these things."

Leah stopped Nell beside Beauty and allowed her to drop her nose to the ground and begin nuzzling at the grass.

She hated to have this conversation here, Leah thought regretfully, but there were things she wanted to tell Marc and now her opportunity had come.

"For some time, I've been thinking about the way we've dealt with Ariana, and I must admit, I've been wrong about something."

"Thank goodness you see that!"

"I've given in too easily where she's concerned."

"*What?*"

"I'm more than just a nanny. You knew that when you hired me. I've had a great deal of training in working with people like Ariana. As a professional, I feel I haven't been doing my job."

"What's that supposed to mean?"

"I've been considering you, not Ariana," Leah explained quietly. "I think that pleasing you is what I've wanted most. But sometimes I can't, not if I want to do what's best for your sister."

"Thanks a lot." Sarcasm dripped from every word, but Leah ignored it.

"Too many times," she went on, "I've yielded to your wishes when I've truly believed that another approach would have been better for Ariana. I apologize. I've worried too much about making you happy."

"Am I supposed to be grateful? It seems to me life hasn't always been so terrific since you instituted your changes."

"I realize that. Melanie said—" Leah bit off the sentence, mentally berating herself for being so careless.

"You talked to Melanie about this?"

"Apparently *you* have."

"We've been thrown together on a case. It's hardly surprising if I occasionally mention my home life." He looked at her suspiciously. "I doubt you have such an excuse."

"I have no excuse other than she came to the house to talk."

"She came to my house? To talk about my sister and me? How . . . interesting."

So he would tolerate Melanie's meddling in his life, but not give her, Leah, permission to do what she was trained to do!

Irritated, Leah kicked Nell's sides with her heels. "Last one to the halfway point on the trail is a rotten egg!" She leaned forward and encouraged Nell into a gallop. For once, she, not Marc, had the edge. Though Marc gave a yell and followed, he couldn't catch up.

The halfway point of the trail was marked by a vine-covered Victorian gazebo. Leah had already slid off Nell's back and was tethering her to a post when Marc caught up.

"No fair, you had a head start!" His skin was ruddy and his hair windblown. He dismounted with grace and agility.

"Sorry. I felt the need for a little...air." Leah climbed the steps to the gazebo and sat on the wooden bench.

"And a little space—that didn't have me in it?"

"I suppose so."

"I can always count on you to be honest, can't I?"

"It's a flaw of mine," Leah said.

"Not necessarily."

Much to her surprise, he didn't sound angry. He didn't *act* angry, either, as he sat on the bench beside her and rested his arm on the back railing. His fingers played with her wild tangle of hair.

"You look like you rode into this place on a stiff breeze."

"Got a comb? I can fix it in a hurry."

"I like your hair like that. It's...sexy."

Leah stared at him, dumbfounded. "Sexy? Why, Marc Adams, how you're talking! And to the nanny, too!"

He grinned and moved his hand to the nape of her neck. "That's not all I plan to do to the nanny. Come here." He placed his mouth over hers and explored the softness of her lips. After that, he dragged a trail of tiny kisses across her cheek to her ear. There, he followed the delicate outline of her earlobe, nibbling carefully around her diamond earring. Leah shivered blissfully.

"Are you really trying to make me happy?" he asked.

Leah pulled away to look at his full sensuous lips. "What are you talking about?"

"A few minutes ago you said that often you were trying to please me rather than follow your conscience. Is that true?"

"Yes, but—"

"Why?" He took the tip of her ear between his teeth and bit gently.

Leah squirmed even closer to him. "Because I want you to be happy."

"But why?"

"Because I'm not objective any more. I feel too much...emotion where you're concerned." If he didn't stop tormenting her, she was going to lose control and tell him exactly what she felt—admiration, respect, *love*.

His thumb slipped beneath the collar of her shirt to caress her shoulder, and Leah's breath caught in her throat.

"I've done a lot of thinking about Ariana. Maybe I have been overreacting. Maybe the center is a good place for her to spend some time."

"You mean she can go back?"

"On certain conditions. You drive her there and escort her inside before you park the car. You let Alf Orenson know when you're coming so he can be watching for you. And she doesn't have to go every day. Just once in a while to start."

"That is, if there still *is* a center," Leah said gloomily. "I imagine their legal bills are running them into the ground."

"Oh, I think they'll be all right."

"Sure. Easy for you to say. You aren't involved. Anyway, how would you—" Leah stopped and gazed at him with wide eyes. "How *would* you know what's going on with the center?"

"Legal grapevine. That sort of thing. Now, back to what we were doing..."

Leah pressed her hands against his chest. "You *do* know something about the center, don't you? Marc Adams, what have you been keeping from me?"

He gave her his most innocent look. "Let's just say I did a little research for them."

"You worked for the center?"

"It didn't take much. I only had to check out some zoning laws. The area where the center's located has been zoned for schools. If a school for 'normal' children were to open at that address, it couldn't be stopped. What it boiled down to was that the neighborhood residents didn't want a school for the handicapped in their area."

A satisfied expression glimmered briefly on his face. "Once the neighborhood opposition realized they might be treading on something very touchy—like discriminatory acts against the handicapped—things settled down nicely. I believe the center will be there as long as Ariana needs it." His words were muffled by the joyous kiss Leah planted on his lips.

"Oh, thank you! Thank you! Thank you! It'll be so much better for your sister! Oh, Marc, this is wonderful news! You've made me so happy!" Leah jumped up from the gazebo bench and twirled around. When Nell looked up to see what the commotion was about, Leah threw her arms around the horse's neck and gave a squeeze. "Let's go right home and tell Ariana!"

Marc stared sourly at Nell and Leah. "Fine thanks I get," he muttered. "I give the lady what she asks for and she hugs the horse!" He stood and sauntered over this mount. "Next time I give her good news, I'm going to get what *I* want first!"

CHAPTER TWELVE

"I'M TAKING ARIANA to the center today," Leah announced. "There's a fifth-anniversary celebration, and Ariana doesn't want to miss it."

"She loves going there, doesn't she?" Mrs. Bright's eyes misted. "I've never seen her so happy."

Leah nodded, then glanced at her watch. "We'd better hurry. I want to talk to the coordinator at the center about...something." Leah didn't admit she'd made an appointment to discuss group homes. It was a precautionary move; if the subject ever came up, she wanted to be prepared.

She and Marc hadn't really talked since the afternoon at the gazebo, and though she felt she'd secured a victory for Ariana, she still didn't know where she stood with Marc.

She knew he liked her, but apparently he also liked Melanie Dean. He hadn't seemed upset to learn that his assistant was meddling in his personal life. That fact provoked Leah. Melanie was her competition, and Leah felt outclassed.

"IS THIS A FLOWER or a weed?" Ariana wondered late the next afternoon as she and Leah worked in the garden. When Leah turned to answer, Ariana thrust the tiny plant, roots and all, in Leah's face.

"Fortunately that's a weed. What were you planning to do if it had been a flower?"

"Put it back?"

Leah chuckled as she wiped her soil-caked hands on her jeans. "I think it's time to go inside and clean up. Your brother will be home soon. We have more dirt on ourselves than we've left in the garden."

"You look funny," Ariana giggled. "Dirty. And messy."

"Thanks a bunch. I'll head straight for the shower." Leah dumped the gardening tools into a plastic bucket, picked up the flowers she'd cut and headed for the house. Ariana trailed behind, humming to herself.

"I'm going to put these in a vase, then I'll be right up," Leah called. With the bucket in one hand and the flowers in the other, Leah strode into the living room.

"How cute. The nanny even gardens." Melanie Dean rose from the piano bench, swathed in black velvet from the creamy rise of her breasts to the elegant curve of her calf. The strapless evening gown she wore accentuated her best attributes. A large diamond on a gold chain nestled at her throat and a diamond stud graced each ear. Her dark hair was swept back in a stunning French roll.

"I'm sorry," Leah mumbled. "I didn't know anyone was here. I..." She backed toward the door and directly into Marc. As he put his hands on her shoulders and spun her around, Leah was mortified to feel a blush creep into her cheeks.

"Careful," he said. "I just changed my clothes. And you're a bit...dirty." He held her at arm's length and regarded her curiously. Leah wished he wouldn't touch her. It was so much more difficult to think when he touched her. She felt her knees grow weak. He was so handsome! His dark hair was slightly damp and swept away from his high, intelligent brow, except for the errant lock which had dared to slip out of place. His dusky eyes were filled with laughter.

"I...I just brought in some flowers," Leah stammered. "I didn't realize you were home. I usually watch for you—"

Leah wanted to bite off her tongue! Why give either of them any hint of her love for Marc? Until—and unless—he declared his feelings and intentions, she was determined to protect herself. Unfortunately, with each passing day, that was becoming more and more difficult to do.

"Melanie and I have a business dinner to attend. Since we've been working together so much lately, I thought it might be nice to relax over a drink."

"Don't let me bother you." Leah squirmed out of his grip and moved toward the hall, dropping little clumps of dirt from her clothes as she went. She gave a sheepish shrug. "I'll come back later and vacuum up after myself."

Marc smiled oddly, as if he found something amusing. Leah, however, saw no humor in the situation. With a final glance at Melanie, she escaped from the room.

By the time Leah heard Marc's car leave, her grimy clothes were sloshing in the washing machine, and she was soaking in a tub of frothy bubbles.

"I could be as gorgeous as Melanie Dean," she muttered. "If I had the time…and the money…and the… Oh, rats!" Groaning she sank deeper into the water.

"Leah?" Mrs. Bright pushed open the bedroom door after a tentative knock. "Are you still up?"

"Come in," Leah said, giving a catlike stretch. "I need a break." She tossed the notebook she was holding aside. "I was tinkering with floor plans for my office."

"Is it ready?" the housekeeper asked. She perched on the edge of the bed and primly laced her fingers together.

"Soon, although it seems that there're a million details to iron out. I don't want to open my doors until everything's perfect. I've waited this long, so a few more weeks one way or the other won't matter."

"What about Ariana? What will she do without you?"

"Ariana will manage just fine. She's learned so much."

Ariana's world had expanded far beyond this house. In the past few weeks, Leah had accompanied her to the Washington Monument and the Lincoln Memorial. They'd gazed at the White House and strolled through the zoo. Marc had begun taking his sister out for dinner, and with each event Ariana's confidence grew. She was now capable of spending her entire day at the center—when Marc allowed it. Ariana no longer needed a nanny. Leah had worked herself out of a job.

It was ending; her time in the Adams household was drawing to a close. Her new business was almost ready to open, and Ariana didn't need her anymore. Marc and Melanie had found each other.

When Mrs. Bright left, Leah sighed and pulled the goose-down comforter up to her chin. Marc and Leah. That was the one thing she hadn't accomplished.

She spent a restless night and awoke feeling tired and unrefreshed. She dressed quickly, gazing out her window at a gray, drizzly day. Then she hurried downstairs, her mind skittering from one unpleasant reality to another, including Ariana's appointment that morning.

She hated to bring up touchy subjects at breakfast, but this was unavoidable. She waited until Marc was on his second cup of coffee. "I need your help."

"You? Asking for help?" The dimple in his cheek quirked with amusement. "I never thought I'd see the day!"

"Ariana has an appointment at the dentist's. Do you want me to drive her or—"

Marc shook his head emphatically. "I'll do it. She can be difficult about this. Besides, the weather isn't good." There had been an early-morning storm, which had subsided into a bone-chilling mist. The house felt damp and gloomy, matching Leah's mood. To make matters worse, Ariana's response to the announcement of her dental appointment was exactly what Leah had feared.

"I don't want to go! No!" Huge tears rolled down the girl's cheeks as Leah and Marc cajoled her out the door. "It hurts!"

"It doesn't hurt, honey," Leah comforted. "This is just a checkup."

"It hurts." Ariana clawed at Marc's cashmere coat sleeve. "Don't make me go, Marc. Please?"

Ariana protested so long and loud that finally Marc had to lift her bodily into the car, his expression strained but resolute. Leah could hear Ariana crying even after the doors were closed.

To distract herself, Leah dug out some paper and a pen. For the next two hours she designed ads for the Nonesuch Nannies. The time passed with excruciating slowness.

"Aren't they ever going to get back?" Leah wondered aloud. "They've been gone for hours."

"I hope they didn't have to wait in the dentist's office," Mrs. Bright said worriedly. "Once, Ariana started to hyperventilate and the poor little thing nearly fainted. I can't understand why they aren't—"

The doorbell interrupted her, and they both rushed to answer it. Leah got there first. Her heart raced when she saw the uniformed police officer.

"Mrs. Adams?" he asked politely.

"I'm Leah Brock, an employee of Mr. Adams's. Is something wrong?" A ripple of icy fear washed over her, leaving her skin feeling cold and clammy.

"There's been an accident involving Mr. Adams and a young lady..." he read emotionlessly from his notes.

Leah clutched the door for support. "Marc! Ariana!"

"The report says that another car hydroplaned on the wet road and sideswiped Mr. Adams's car."

Leah grabbed the officer's arm, her nails digging into the crisply pressed jacket. "Are they...." she couldn't finish.

He patted her hand. "All right? Yes. There were no fatalities. In fact, the accident could have been much worse, considering the condition of the roads and the amount of traffic. If you'd allow me to take you to the hospital..."

Leah turned to Mrs. Bright. "I'll call you as soon as I know what's happened. If either of them can be released I'll bring them home in a taxi. Otherwise I'll stay."

Mrs. Bright nodded and wrung her hands. "I can't bear to sit at home and not know what's happened." Impulsively Leah reached for the older woman and they clung to each other for support.

"I'll call you," Leah promised. "Don't worry."

"MR. ADAMS IS in room 304." The nurse spoke softly as she pointed down a long, stark corridor. "You may go in for five minutes. No more. The doctor wants to hold him for observation tonight."

"His sister..." Leah began, her heart pounding so loudly she barely heard the nurse speak.

"She's downstairs in emergency. I believe she'll be able to go home."

Leah willed herself to walk, not run, down the hall.

The room was dark and quiet. The curtains were drawn, shutting out the gray light. She tiptoed toward the bed, fearful of what she might find. Marc was frighteningly still beneath an ugly green thermal blanket, a pristine bandage wrapped around his head. As Leah drew close, his eyelids fluttered open.

"Leah?"

Gently she touched his hair. "Oh, Marc, you scared us!" Her voice quavered and she stopped, unable to go on, incapable of expressing the turmoil she felt.

"Is Ariana...?"

"Ariana's fine. She's downstairs in the emergency room being examined. The nurse said she could probably go home."

He closed his eyes again and sagged with relief against the pillows. "Thank God. I was afraid..." He paused. "Take care of her, Leah."

"You know I will. Mrs. Bright is waiting at home, too." Leah tried to smile. "If I know her, she's busy cooking all Ariana's favorite foods. We'll be eating lasagna and brownies for weeks."

Marc tried to turn his head and grimaced. "I feel like I've been clubbed with a baseball bat."

Leah leaned over to smooth a stray lock of hair from his eyes and, on impulse, kissed him lightly on the cheek. "You frightened us," she repeated.

One corner of his mouth twisted wryly; it left him looking vulnerable, lovable and very masculine all at the same time. "Sorry. It wasn't planned. We got blindsided."

"So the policeman said. When he came to the door, I thought my heart would stop."

"Don't think about it, Leah. We're all right." His eyes darkened in concern. "Have you seen Ariana?"

"Not yet. I'm going now. I just wanted to see for myself that you were okay." The tenderness and love she felt for him threatened to overwhelm her. She was almost grateful to see a brisk nurse strut into the room carrying a small tray with a thermometer, several bottles and a syringe.

"You'll have to go now," she said. "The doctor has ordered medication for Mr. Adams, and it's going to make him drowsy. We've just been told that Mr. Adams's sister is ready to be released." As she spoke, the nurse deftly pulled the privacy curtains around the bed. Leah spun on her heel and escaped into the hall, hurrying toward the elevators and Ariana.

The girl was a pale ghost of her usual self as she sat on the emergency-room examining table. An ugly bruise colored one temple and her arm was cradled in a white sling.

"Leah!" she wailed and promptly burst into tears.

"It's okay, honey," Leah crooned. "We can go home now."

"Where's Marc? I talked to him in the car, but he wouldn't wake up."

"He's awake now, but the doctor wants him to stay here tonight. He's going to have a very bad headache. I'll bring him home tomorrow. You'll help me take care of him, won't you?"

Ariana nodded obediently and allowed a nurse to help her from the examining table and into a wheelchair. Leah made a quick phone call to Mrs. Bright and then they left.

Once they were in the taxi, Ariana began to babble anxiously about the accident, explaining in her simple, unsophisticated way how a car had careered out of nowhere and slammed into them. She clung painfully to Leah's hand for the entire trip home.

As Leah listened, she realized how close she'd come to losing the two people she loved most. She knew, too, that she loved Marc more than ever, in spite of the differences between them. In spite of the fact that those differences meant he would never be hers.

CHAPTER THIRTEEN

WOULD VISITING HOURS never begin?

Leah yawned. She'd hardly slept the night before. Her brain had been too full of thoughts of Marc and the accident. And the morning had been no easier. She'd received word that her office would be ready for occupancy in less than two weeks, which meant she'd be leaving the Adams household soon.

"You may go in now," the nurse said. Leah bolted down the hallway without waiting for further prompting.

Marc sat in the cushioned chair by his hospital window, his eyes dark against his ashen face.

"Hi." The single word seemed an effort.

"Hi, yourself." Leah shifted awkwardly from her right foot to her left as words escaped her.

"I should have told you to bring me some clean clothes," he joked weakly. "Mine are pretty muddy."

"You'll look fine to me."

More than fine. You look…precious, so very precious to me.

"I can go home today. But the doctor hasn't been around to release me yet."

"Are you sure you're ready? You don't look very strong." Leah sank into a nearby chair and twisted her hands in her lap, wishing she could offer him more comfort.

"It's quieter at home. Here, they wake me up at three in the morning to see if I need a sleeping pill." A faint smile creased his handsome face, and Leah resisted the urge to touch his lips with the tip of her finger.

The rush of emotion left her feeling awkward and self-conscious. She busied herself rearranging the flowers on the dresser and folding the robe that lay at the foot of the bed. When the room was neat, she sighed and returned to the bed. "I feel so helpless, so... ineffective."

He studied her intently and an amused expression crossed his features. "You might be a lot of things, Leah Brock, but ineffective isn't one of them."

"Do you want to talk about the accident?" Leah asked bluntly, ignoring the way he tried to direct the conversation away from him. "About how you feel? About Ariana? Anything?"

Rather than brushing aside her question, he chose his words with obvious care. "Ariana and I talked on the way home from the dentist—before the accident. She talked about the center. She told me how much she loved going there." Marc drew a ragged breath. "She also told me that some of her friends live in group homes and have jobs."

Leah's palms grew moist as she sensed that Marc was struggling to say something very important. "Go on," she encouraged.

"As we drove, I asked her if she'd like a job someday." He stared pensively out the window, and the bedside clock ticked loudly as the minutes passed. "She told me she'd like to wash dishes the way her friend Kristie does." Marc's voice was controlled and steady, but a sense of wonder shone in his eyes. "She said if she was careful, she thought she could wash dishes without breaking a single one." His shoulders sagged and he looked defeated. "I'm ashamed of myself, Leah."

"Ashamed? You have no reason to feel ashamed."

"Don't I?" Casually Marc ran his finger along Leah's arm to her hand. "I should think you'd have recognized me for what I am, or was, by now."

"What are, or were, you?"

"A snob."

That was the last thing she'd expected him to say. "I don't understand."

"All the time my sister was talking proudly about being capable of holding a job, I wondered what my parents would think if they knew their precious daughter wanted to become a dishwasher." He looked down at his hand and seemed surprised to see Leah's smaller one nestled in it. "My parents would have thought it beneath an Adams to hold a menial job. That's what I've been thinking, too."

"What changed your mind?"

"When I saw that car coming at us—" Marc shuddered "—I knew immediately that I couldn't avoid it. There was no way I could keep either one of us safe." His grip tightened reflexively on Leah's hand. "I realized that I might be killed."

"Oh, Marc," Leah moaned, "don't!"

"It's true. At that same moment, I wondered what would happen to Ariana if I died and she lived. I was wrong, Leah. Ariana *does* need a life apart from me. I can't be her entire world. If something happened to me, it would devastate her."

"But nothing did happen. You're fine. You're both fine."

"That doesn't change things. Ariana should experience life as fully as possible. You've been right all along. I'm sorry I fought you, but I've been so damned torn between the promise I made to my parents and the perfect sense you always make when it comes to Ariana." His voice was husky with concern. "Have I hurt her, Leah? I didn't mean to."

"Of course not! It isn't too late for Ariana. She's a beautiful girl who feels loved and secure. She's stronger for that, not weaker." Leah reached up and stroked the silken strands of his hair. "The people at the center would be delighted to have her around whenever she wants to come. If she wants a job, they'll find her one. If you decide to let her stay in a group home, they'll help you then, too. You needn't move too quickly. You've come a long way already."

He studied her with a look so intense that Leah began to squirm. Finally he raised a hand to her jaw and stroked it gently.

"There's a flip side to this, you know." His expression changed like quicksilver, and Leah felt a responsive flutter in her stomach. "If my sister is free to experience life, that means I'm free, too."

"Oh?" she murmured cautiously. He seemed decidedly healthy. Healthy and downright lustful. Silently he pulled her toward him for a thorough and passionate kiss.

When he lifted his head, a smile had crept into his eyes. "I think I'd like to go home. There are some . . . things I've thought about doing for a long time. Now might be the time to start."

Anticipation shot through Leah as he stood up and tossed away the blanket that had covered his lap. "Where are my clothes?" he demanded. "I can't go anywhere without trousers."

"You certainly can't. There's probably no back in that gown you're wearing."

She found his clothes in the nearby closet and held them just out of reach. "Aren't you going to thank me?"

"Come here and I'll thank you." He drew her close and his mouth pressed against hers. Leah clung to him, her fingers caressing his warm skin, oblivious to the world around them until a whiny, petulant sound assaulted them.

"I came as soon as I—Marc?"

Leah's lips were warm and swollen as she stared at Melanie Dean standing in the doorway. Marc drew a steadying breath near her ear.

Melanie gaped at him and her face flushed a dangerous red. "What's going on in here?"

Marc's voice held a highly amused note. "Nothing you need to be concerned about."

"But Marc..." Melanie didn't finish; she just turned and walked from the room. As the door closed behind her, Mark and Leah could hear her muttering. "The man was just in an accident. Can that be *good* for him?"

Marc chuckled. "Can anything be *better* for an injured man?

Boldly Leah pulled him close to resume their kiss. "Only this," she said.

CHAPTER FOURTEEN

A FESTIVE CLUSTER of balloons floated in the corner of the dining room as Leah decorated the table with noisemakers, streamers and brightly colored paper napkins. The final touch was a shiny foil hat at each place setting.

Marc carried a teetering pile of packages into the room. He dumped them on the table and gathered Leah into his arms, burying his nose in her fragrant hair.

"Are we ready? Ariana's upstairs having a fit because she can't help prepare for her own birthday party."

"Frankly I'd rather you and I have a celebration of our own. A little fruit, a little cheese, a little wine, a little..." His caresses left no doubt in Leah's mind about what else he wanted.

"Well, I guess we're committed to this. Mrs. Bright is putting the candles on the cake. Looks like Ariana will have a regular bonfire on her hands. Her friends from the center should be impressed."

Marc drew his hands away and settled them on his own hips. "Ariana is eighteen years old. It's hard to believe, isn't it?" As he stared past the festive table toward the gardens, his expression grew pensive. "I thought I knew exactly what life held for Ariana." He gave Leah a faintly scolding look. "And then you came along."

"Me?" she said with feigned innocence.

"Yes, you. Instead of a meek quiet child, my sister has ended up being some kind of... activist or something." He reached for her again and gently kissed her.

"I don't think learning to be independent borders on activism."

"In this house it does." He traced a pattern across her lips and down her neck, pausing at a particularly vulnerable spot on her collarbone.

"Ariana is having a birthday and moving into a group home, not picketing at the White House." She felt his lips curve into a smile over her own.

"Same thing," he muttered stubbornly. "It's all unexpected."

"Where's my party?" a voice from the doorway demanded. Ariana stood there in her birthday finery—a denim skirt and an oversize sweater with a huge pink teddy bear on the front. Her blue eyes twinkled and she smiled as she said teasingly, "No kissing at my party!"

Marc released Leah and sauntered toward his sister. "Not even a kiss for the birthday girl?" Ariana giggled and allowed him to give her cheek a noisy smack.

When the doorbell rang, Ariana jumped away with an excited squeal. "They're here!"

"They" were several of Ariana's friends from the center, all transported to the house by the minivan used for special outings. Mrs. Macatee had been invited to chaperon the group and help with the celebration.

Lily, Brenda, Kristie and Lynn were all dressed for the party, and when Ariana appeared, they screeched with delight.

"Did the decibel level just go up in here?" Marc said, shaking his head.

"Teenage girls," Mrs. Macatee explained. "Noisiest creatures on the face of the earth. And the excitement has barely started."

Her prediction was accurate. The five girls giggled through the video Leah had rented, swapped private jokes and oohed over Ariana's gifts as she unwrapped them.

Through it all, Marc was patient, indulgent and a little awestruck. As he watched the gift-opening ritual, Leah slipped up behind him and slid her arms around his waist. He rested his hands over hers and continued to watch the unwrapping, with torn paper and discarded ribbon scattered everywhere.

"She's just like any other kid having friends over for a birthday party, isn't she?"

"Of course," Leah murmured. "That's because she *is* a kid. And like any other kid, she deserves parties."

"You were right, and I—and my mother—were wrong, Leah. Hiding her away from the world to protect her wasn't what she needed at all. Friends, experiences—those are the things that will help her grow."

"Yes and no." As Leah moved to stand beside him, he draped his arm possessively around her shoulders. "She needs protection, too."

"Look, Leah, Marc! I got makeup!" Ariana held up a box containing tubes of lip gloss and blusher.

"Who gave you that?" Marc growled.

"It's very light," Leah pleaded. "You won't even be able to tell she has it on. It'll be fun for her, Marc."

Leah never heard Marc's answer, because Mrs. Bright entered, carrying a huge birthday cake. Ariana clapped her hands and hurried to her spot at the table. "Let's eat!"

It was hours before Marc and Leah found themselves alone in the living room once again.

"Where is she?" Marc looked around suspiciously. "I don't want to be caught kissing twice." He lifted his eyebrows. "But I think I'll have to take the chance."

"Last I looked, Ariana was sound asleep on her bed wearing every birthday gift she received, including two sweaters, lip gloss, a baseball cap and snow boots."

"Do you think the boots were too much? I want to be sure she's warm when she goes to work . . ."

"We'll see her every day, Marc. After all, she has a job in my building. I'll pick her up at the group home and bring her to work with me." In a stroke of good luck, Leah had heard about a part-time job shredding paper for the businesses in the building. Ariana was delighted to be working at a "real" job, and Marc was relieved to know that Leah would be close at hand. At noon, Marc would join Leah for lunch and return Ariana to the center. Evenings would be spent at the home she shared with her friends and the group-home supervisors.

With a gusty sigh, he sank into one of the leather chairs and pulled Leah onto his lap. She buried her hands beneath his jacket and curled her fingers around his lean, warm torso.

"Ever since the day you walked into this household," Marc said, "I've been outfoxed, outmaneuvered and outorganized. Did you know that?"

Leah breathed deeply, inhaling the after-shave he wore. "Nonsense. You were cold, formal and intimidating. My only goal in this household was survival."

"Survival of the fittest," Marc said, smiling. "That's you." With his finger, he traced a pattern across her forehead and down the short straight line of her nose, stopping at her lips which he stroked lightly. "Besides, if it's so awful here, why are you planning to stay?"

"Because you asked me to marry you," Leah said simply. "How could I say no? I wouldn't want to hurt your feelings."

"You mean you're going to start listening to what *I* say? And doing what I ask?"

"Oh, no," Leah purred. "That would be too easy. I think a marriage should be . . . exciting. If I became predictable now, you might lose interest in me."

"Doubtful," Marc assured her. "After the past few months, I'd appreciate a little predictability."

Leah placed her index fingers on her temples and closed her eyes.

"I predict that there will be a wedding in this house," she intoned. "I predict that Mrs. Bright will be in her element making petits fours and miniature cream puffs and baking the world's grandest wedding cake. I predict that Ariana will be my maid of honor." Leah opened her eyes, caught the tip of her tongue between her teeth and smiled. "How's that for predictability?" Leah pulled a piece of paper from her pocket and handed it to Marc. "I almost forgot. Ariana asked me to give you this."

He opened the note, which held a roughly drawn heart with the words MARC LOVE LEAH in the center.

"My sister is certainly perceptive." Marc murmured as he unfastened the top button of Leah's blouse. He undid a second button and a third, then leaned to kiss the soft skin beneath. When he looked up, his eyes were hazy with desire.

"What's happened to me, Leah? You wove a spell over me from the moment you entered my life." He nipped playfully at her shoulder, and she shivered with pleasure. "You must be a magician."

"Not guilty," she told him. "It was Ariana's magic, not mine, that brought us together."

"But she's not here now," he whispered huskily, trapping her hand between his hands and kissing her hard and long, "and the magic is stronger than ever."

The magic *was* stronger, Leah mused as she melted into his arms. And she was sure it would last forever.

HARLEQUIN PROUDLY PRESENTS A
DAZZLING CONCEPT IN ROMANCE FICTION

 One small town,
twelve terrific love stories

JOIN US FOR A YEAR IN THE FUTURE OF TYLER

Each book set in Tyler is a self-contained love story; together,
the twelve novels stitch the fabric of the community.

LOSE YOUR HEART TO TYLER!

Join us for the second TYLER book, BRIGHT HOPES, by
Pat Warren, available in April.

*Former Olympic track star Pam Casals arrives in Tyler to
coach the high school team. Phys ed instructor Patrick
Kelsey is first resentful, then delighted. And rumors fly about
the dead body discovered at the lodge.*

If you missed the first title, WHIRLWIND, and would like to order it, send your name, address, zip or postal code, along with a check or money order for $3.99 plus 75¢ postage and handling ($1.00 in Canada), payable to Harlequin Reader Service to:

In the U.S.
3010 Walden Avenue
P.O. Box 1325
Buffalo, NY 14269-1325

In Canada
P.O. Box 609
Fort Erie, Ontario
L2A 5X3

Please specify book title(s) with your order.
Canadian residents add applicable federal and provincial taxes.

TYLER-2

Following the success of WITH THIS RING,
Harlequin cordially invites you to enjoy the
romance of the wedding season with

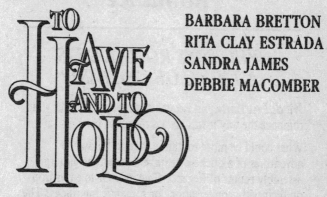

BARBARA BRETTON
RITA CLAY ESTRADA
SANDRA JAMES
DEBBIE MACOMBER

A collection of romantic stories that celebrate the joy,
excitement, and mishaps of planning that special day
by these four award-winning Harlequin authors.

**Available in April at your favorite Harlequin
retail outlets.**

THTH

Harlequin Regency Romance™

WHO SAYS ROMANCE IS A THING OF THE PAST?

We do! At Harlequin Regency Romance, we offer you romance the way it was always meant to be.

What could be more romantic than to follow the adventures of a duchess or duke through the glittering assembly rooms of Regency England? Or to eavesdrop on their witty conversations or romantic interludes? The music, the costumes, the ballrooms and the dance will sweep you away to a time when pleasure was a priority and privilege a prerequisite.

If you are longing for the good old days when falling in love still meant something very special, then come to Harlequin Regency Romance—romance with a touch of class.

RRG

Jackson: Honesty was his policy...
and the price he demanded of the woman
he loved.

THE LAST HONEST MAN
by Leandra Logan
Temptation #393, May 1992

All men are not created equal. Some are
rough around the edges. Tough-minded but
tenderhearted. Incredibly sexy. The tempting
fulfillment of every woman's fantasy.

When it's time to fight for what they believe in,
to win that special woman, our Rebels and Rogues
are heroes at heart. Twelve Rebels and Rogues,
one each month in 1992, only from
Harlequin Temptation!

If you missed the previous Rebels & Rogues titles and would like to order them, please send $2.99 for *The Private Eye* (#377), *The Hood* (#381), *The Outsider* (#385) or *The Wolf* (#389), plus 75¢ postage and handling ($1.00 in Canada) for each book ordered, payable to Harlequin Reader Service to:

In the U.S.	In Canada
3010 Walden Avenue	P.O. Box 609
P.O. Box 1325	Fort Erie, Ontario
Buffalo, NY 14269-1325	L2A 5X3

Please specify book title(s) with your order.
Canadian residents add applicable federal and provincial taxes.

RR-4-E-R

Janet Dailey Americana

Janet Dailey's perennially popular Americana series continues with more exciting states!

Don't miss this romantic tour of America through fifty favorite Harlequin Presents novels, each one set in a different state, and researched by Janet and her husband, Bill.

A journey of a lifetime in one cherished collection.

April titles	**#29 NEW HAMPSHIRE**
	Heart of Stone
	#30 NEW JERSEY
	One of the Boys

If you missed your state or would like to order any other states that have already been published, send your name, address, zip or postal code, along with a check or money order for $3.99 plus 75¢ postage and handling ($1.00 in Canada) for each book ordered, payable to Harlequin Reader Service to:

In the U.S.

3010 Walden Avenue
P.O. Box 1325
Buffalo, NY 14269-1325

In Canada

P.O. Box 609
Fort Erie, Ontario
L2A 5X3

Please specify book title(s) with your order.
Canadian residents add applicable federal and provincial taxes.

JD-APR